About the Author

Craig Minto was born in Sheffield in 1966. He has always loved the writing and illustration of his stories. Writing began as an enjoyable hobby but then Craig went on to college and university where he studied Creative Writing, graduating in 2011 with a BA Degree.

With all my love and thanks to Dad, Yvonne and Janine
X

Not forgetting
Bob and Shanie X

Craig Minto

HOMELESS ANGELS

AUSTIN MACAULEY
PUBLISHERS LTD.

A CIP catalogue record for this title is available from the British Library.

ISBN 9781784555122 (Paperback)
ISBN 9781784555139 (Hardback)
ISBN 9781784555146 (E-Book)

www.austinmacauley.com

First Published (2017)
Austin Macauley Publishers Ltd.
25 Canada Square
Canary Wharf
London
E14 5LQ

1

GARY

Part One

They don't know who I am. Even if they did; I doubt they would care!

I slept on the damp bench in the shadows of Sheffield Cathedral. Last night the bench was a meeting place for me, Stan and Jane.

We didn't need to beg very much that day; I remember. Jane had twenty quid. A kind soul gave her this. He was a 'posh un, and all'. She said she had been crouched in the alley by the side of the old Court House. He gently placed the purple note in her hand.

But Stan and Jane told me they were to hitch to London. So I reckoned I might not be able to share their wonderful company for a while.

A couple of weeks later I'm in another part of the city. One of my favourite haunts, up by the museum, the one overlooking the boating lake and the bandstand. A place I like to make me sen comfortable. It is nice and cosy there, a safe haven from this hard, cruel world.

The big strong oak doors take some forcing open. They are all warped and stuck together.

But once I'm inside the old red sleeping bag and crashed out on the padded, ripped seating; it's grand.

It was the middle of January though. The wind's bitter, the cold bloody cuts me up. I am just drifting off into a lovely bit of kip, when a white beam of light flows in harshly through the broken windows. There is a tremendous crash. The door bangs to the floor. They both burst in.

"Stand up!" the copper shouts sharply like.

"Stand up! Get thee sen tidy!"

The next I know I'm taken down to the cop shop; the big one on Queen's Hill in the middle of town. The other copper who burst in is a lass. She din't say 'owt, but if looks were found to be killers, I'd have had me lot, if you know what I mean?

They question me all about the crime for two days and nights. They humiliated me, reminding me with cruelty of my glory days back in 1982; on that July day in Madrid, Spain, of being the local Sheffield hero, for years after.

I was England's goalkeeper who won a World Cup winner's medal, who shook hands with the King of Spain; proudly smiling with joy as he presented me with the prize.

Growling, taunting me. The police told me none of the acclaim was deserved. Telling me I was no local hero after all, that I was a nobody, to the city of my birth. The city I was raised in.

They would eventually charge me.

Five years on the police still think I am the culprit; they still insist I am a murderer.

I continue to cry my innocence that I had nothing whatsoever to do with the whole tragedy!

Poor old Stan! Well he never did reach London ever again. He was to be found stabbed, a brutal killing behind the Cathedral, a place where we had all spent joyful times, singing the old songs, smoking and drinking the old cheap cider. Happy! We would reminisce of our heady, halcyon days, our carefree times of 1960s London and Sheffield.

It's not so bad in the clink though. Not really. It's an improvement on being homeless. In a way it is. But I didn't mind begging. I had safe havens to kip in. The winters were cruel at times. The nasty northern wind cut my legs up, legs which already ailed me.

I've just returned to my cell. We have all been allowed to watch TV. Only for a couple of hours though. A prison perk. If that's what you call it? They showed a clip from the '66 World Cup Final. The last minute saves. I thwart the West German centre forward leaping high and majestic like! Clawing the bright orange Casey ball from hitting the netting behind me!

But the other prisoners don't have a clue who I am. I'm really glad in a way!

2

STAN

Gary and Jane saved me. I had some of the best days of my life, days of having nothing at all. But I had their friendship. Back when the Sheffield streets were my home.

How did I come to be homeless?

A question I asked myself. One I've asked many times.

I came from Clapham, the South London of my birth. That was back in 2007. Well I became homeless overnight that year. It seemed to happen that quickly!

The firm had sent me up north to sort out an account, one which was proving difficult. They needed my help up in Sheffield that July time.

Jack Saunders, my boss, had said to me on the Friday.

"Stan, our Sheffield office has got some probs!'" He always said probs, and it bloody annoyed the hell out of me.

"The bloody Spalding account's in a mess, lad," he said, harshly.

"Can you buzz on up there by train Monday, and see if you can help 'em out?"

He was a funny old sod Saunders. I always thought he had no time for me back then. Well not up until that Friday.

We had never said more than a couple of words to each other in all the ten years I'd been at Taylor and Saunders Accountants.

I always thought Saunders didn't believe in me that much, that my work was of no benefit to the firm. Not really!

But for God's sake! I wished I'd never agreed to take that train, up north that Monday morning.

2007 had been a real trial for me. It had begun when my mother Kate had passed away. Her brave battle against leukaemia had beaten us both. Then in the March, Julia couldn't deal with it all, with my anger, depression and foul moods. All triggered by Kate's passing, our decade of marriage dissolving, just like my spit in the London rains.

Working at Taylor and Saunders was hell as ever. I was walking on broken eggshells every day, trying to please the old bastards.

Ernie Taylor wasn't a bad bloke really. He was one for a quiet life. As long as I got on with my work that was. He was pretty laid back and easy going to be fair. But Jack was a miserly, cold-hearted old sod most of the time.

The pay I got was pitiful for all the hours God sent that I put in. So when Saunders was kind to me I'm proper bowled over. I had never been to Sheffield. So I thought, me lucks on the up for once!

I jumped on the morning train out of St. Pancras Station. Taking up an isolated seat where I stuck my head in my paperback, an autobiography of Gordon Banks. I had heard somewhere once, he had been born somewhere Sheffield way, I think?

But my peace was disturbed. My peaceful journey to that city of steel destroyed.

I find myself caught up in a bloody domestic! One that I had no business getting involved with at all!

A couple got on at Leicester and sat themselves opposite me, a table separating us. They were both pissed when they got in the carriage. Posh folk. She was blonde haired, make up clouted on with a trowel. Scarlet red lipstick smeared all over her mush, face I mean, wearing a black jacket and pink silk blouse and short, figure hugging black skirt.

Her bloke was a thin sort! He was pasty faced, wearing a chocolate, shitty brown suit. He had these pointy brown shoes on. He looked a clown.

Anyway they are well pissed by the time we get to the station at Chesterfield. I'd only managed to read a little of Banksy's life story, since boarding in London.

Then old thin, pasty, clown shoes stands up, slaps this tart hard across the face. She punches him hard back as retaliation.

Like the idiot I am? I jump out of me seat. To stop 'em half killing each other. Cans of cider, bottles of wine and fag packets fly off all over the place. I ended up brawling with old pasty face clown, in the aisle of the carriage.

The transport police were alerted. They escorted all three of us to the 'cop shop' in Sheffield city centre.

I never did make that meeting. The Spalding account never did get sorted. Not by me anyway. I end up twiddling my thumbs. Nursing a broken nose and swollen cheek bone. Not to mention my dented pride. We were all then detained overnight in prison cells.

The result of all this mayhem was I was given the push from Taylor and Saunders Chartered Accountants! Given my cards by that old ogre Jack Saunders, he gave me my cards and told me not to expect a reference. So my future looked bleak. As far as work was concerned anywhere else anyhow!

I never did return to my flat in Clapham. I did return to 'good old' London Town though with a girl called Jane later on.

I was to quickly descend into a life of heavy drinking, of not giving a shit about myself, or anyone else for that matter. I supped all kinds of booze on the streets of Sheffield.

Jane introduced me to Gary. We all three of us were to look out for each other from then on.

By the harshest of winters of 2009 we both were losing touch with Gary. Jane asked all over town. Asking the street folk or anyone who cared. Who had ever given him a quid or two or a cigarette or food anytime?

The last time Jane and I hooked up with Gary I made a decision.

I hitched back to London with the memory of the last time we had both seen Gary, when we had all had a great time, in the shadows of Sheffield Cathedral that January day.

3

JANE

Gary wasn't in a good place when we met. I mean he was a real mess, but then so was I!

"Hello, Mr!" I said. Cautious as he was someone I thought I may need to be wary of.

It was around midnight that Christmas Eve 2007 I think. I always loved to settle down on the big strong seat, the one in front of Sheffield Cathedral. Feeling safe in the shadows, wrapped up in my big red duvet, my hoodie over my face. Duvet and hoodie around me to stifle a bitterly cold Sheffield wind.

The tall, gaunt, dark haired man was sat on the bench. Staring, looking far into the distance. A can of strong, cheap and lousy cider in his lap, spilling out over his shoes, saturating his ripped, torn and reddened sore toes, peeking out from the blackness of his trainers.

"Oh hiya, Mrs! You ok?" the man asked me. His tone was dull. He mumbled the words.

An hour or so later I found this poorly man to be called Gary. He was a local, from Sheffield.

Gary had been born in a small town to the north of the city. He mentioned he had once played professional football, but had fallen from grace. God knows how? His story a mixed one, muddled up due to the booze he was drinking liberal amounts of.

Gary met Stan. I'd befriended Stan when I first arrived in Sheffield. He had been selling the magazine. *The Street Saviour* was a publication printed by Sheffield Cathedral, one which gave the homeless a helping hand up. Stan would sell the magazine and benefit from a small commission, enough to give him a room in the Hostel in the church dormitories at the back of the Cathedral.

Stan roomed in the church hostel, an initiative to combat the cities horrendous homeless problem. If he could make a steady commission each week a bed was available to him and many other street folk.

Stan had a relapse, a few months before we met. He had some tragic news.

His mother had passed away just before he had arrived in the north from London. She had left a huge hole in his life. Even though a good deal of time had elapsed he would find her loss too much. He would hit the cider and dope again. From time to time, it happens a lot. The streets are a hard isolated existence. You sort yourself out but life begins to hurt you again. You fight back again and again. God knows. We three, Gary, Stan and I, kept trying to do this.

Over the following year we were all to duck and dive. Well enough in fact to all be able to make our lives better. Commission from the *Saviour* magazine meant we could stay, in the dormitory, safe in the hostel and thankful for the small funds and healthier, the three of us. We had a homeless home. Albeit a very temporary one.

But twelve months after hooking up with Gary, my life changed once more. A dramatic, horrendous change occurred.

Stan had won his place in the hostel just shy of Christmas. Those two weeks before, he had got wasted.

On Christmas Eve night all his failings came tumbling out of him. All his rage and anger exploding.

He accused Gary of ripping him off, of cheating him out of earnings from the *Street Saviour*.

Stan threatened me. Claiming I had slept with Gary behind his back, the booze was destroying him.

Decisions, paranoia and self-hatred, all resulted in self destruction. Stan became trouble all right.

Stan had never been more than good friends with Gary. That was the same for me. But he fell for me. He was in love with me. I did not feel the same in that way. Nothing of a sexual or intimate nature happened between us. That was the cold reality of it for us both. Stan lost this grip on the real world. I was saddened to see him change. Change into someone who became a stranger to me.

Leading up to Stan's tragic death, I feared for my own life. Gary had reason to do the same. He was in turmoil, experiencing the loss of strong friendships. He was amazed to witness Stan's decline and crushed not to have his two mates support him, to give him a helping hand.

Stanley Peel was found dead and bleeding. His gaunt, bony body lay slumped at the Cathedral's back door, the door which was the only entrance to *The Street Saviour* and the sanctuary of our homeless hostel.

4

CHARLOTTE

Aimee still does not understand. How do you explain to a five-year-old child where her Dad is? How do I say I haven't a clue where he has disappeared to?

Christmas 2009 was the third one without Gary. The two Christmas Day's before had been lousy.

I had to make the best of things for little Aimee's sake, but she still asked after him. All I thought of to say was "Aimee love Daddy is making us lots of pennies. He is decorating in London for the Queen. Buckingham Palace is a huge house so it will take him a while. When Santa comes next year, he will be back. He will have a lot of pressies for you love."

"Promise, Mummy! Promise he will?"

Aimee would say. But the hurt and puzzled look in her face was heart-breaking for me. That sad and lost look in her eyes was something I was not used to coping with.

"I'll drop the little un off at school love. Then I'm working at Mrs Spooner's place. I've only got her porch to finish painting. I should be done and dusted be' lunch. See you later love. Be good!"

Those were the last words Gary spoke that Friday morning. It was a fortnight before Christmas I remember. He would often say he might be home early. But more often than not his jobs could take longer. Or he would receive a call to quote for more work somewhere else.

But by 8.00 pm that Friday night I was worried. By midnight I was getting frantic. Aimee was fine, I told her that Daddy had arranged to meet up with Uncle Roy. Roy was my kid brother. I told her "Daddy was going to be late home." So she was content to play happily, before falling into a deep sleep around 9.00pm.

The following day was the start of all our worries. That Saturday morning Aimee began to ask so many questions. She began to become fearful and angry.

From that Saturday I was just like my daughter, only hiding my true feelings from her. I dare not speak! I didn't voice the same questions Aimee had. But they were on my mind never the less. My fury was boiling up as well. But I somehow managed to contain it all for her sake. We had both been left high and dry by Gary.

I was burdened with having to deal with the mortgage on the house, all the good natured enquiries from our families, and questions, and offers of help, which in the end became infuriating. Questions which turned to interference after a while for us!

Up until the summer of 2009 Aimee slept in our double bed, the one Gary had built. The one I believed we were happy to retire to every night. The one we were safe in at the close of every month and year. I began to wonder if our fifteen years of marriage had all been a sham!

It had been by no means wedded bliss. Who has a perfect, problem free marriage anyway? But we always worked out our problems. We had good holidays, close friends and Aimee of course. She had made up for all the years Gary had dreamt of having a family. He was the one who seemed so ecstatic when she was born. He was so very happy! I thought he was. So did all our loved ones and our mutual friends.

That first year after Gary left us, Aimee would never sleep soundly. She would toss and turn in our double bed. Waking up in the early hours wanting to play games, read or sometimes she would sob her little heart out. I would hold her close to me. Then she had the habit of crashing out!

She would fall to sleep an hour or so before school time came along. I would need to try and wake her up, to dress her and make our breakfast.

She ended up missing lots of school and sleeping in until midday. The school were great about it all. But she was getting so far behind. I was worried sick for her and myself.

2009 began very well for us. We were more settled and Aimee made a new friend at St. Jude's Primary School.

The Head teacher, Mrs Fletcher, called me one day; she asked if I wouldn't mind visiting her for a chat?

"There is nothing to worry about, Mrs Child's," she said calmly.

"No there is nothing at all wrong."

I was worried, because previously Aimee had been playing up. Just after Gary had left, she'd been very disruptive in school.

Mrs Fletcher was ever so kind. She suggested Aimee might benefit from moving class. To one in which she could get more help. A class where a teacher called Mr Hills had just joined the school.

"You don't have to make up your mind just now, Mrs Childs," Mrs Fletcher said.

"What I thought might help is if you sat in on one of Mr Hill's classes. Maybe have a little chat with him? Or if you prefer I can explain more myself."

"Oh that could be a step forward, Mrs Fletcher," I said, and asked her if I could think this idea of hers over.

"Yes of course, dear. We have all been very much aware at St. Jude's of the difficulties you and Aimee have had recently. I don't want to put any pressure on you both."

"Take as long as you like, dear, I mean really," she said.

"Mummy," Aimee said a couple of days later, after I had spoken with Mrs Fletcher.

"Yes sweetheart," I said.

"Oh Mummy," Aimee continued all excited.

"I've made friends with a new girl at my school. She's so funny, Mummy, and we read books to each other at play time."

"Oh, Aimee, love, that's fantastic, I know you have been a little bit lonely haven't you?" I said trying not to upset her. Because even though Aimee was still only very young, she was so much like her Dad in lots of ways. She was showing signs of being a very independent person who always tried to do things on her own, before asking for any help at all.

The little girl who Aimee had become friends with was called Leah. She was in the new class that Mrs Fletcher had mentioned to me. So when Aimee told me just before her bedtime that night her exciting news, I thought that this was fate in a way.

I secretly think Mrs Fletcher had been keeping an eye on Aimee at school. I also think that she was very concerned for my welfare too. I believe she looked out for me when I collected Aimee after school. Not to interfere in anyway, but I thought this move to Mr Hill's class would be the best for Aimee, leading eventually to a real change of good fortune for us both.

By the Christmas of 2009 Aimee was settled back in her own bedroom.

On Christmas Eve at around 8.00 pm the telephone rang.

Aimee always loved to answer the phone. It hardly ever rang though, only to receive a sales call or wrong number. This was usually the case.

Aimee was about to climb the stairs to bed, but needed to place her glass of milk on the bottom step of the staircase.

She then walked on over to the table by the television set in the corner of our living room and got the shock of her young life!

I was in the kitchen at the time, baking a few mince pies and sausage rolls ready for the next day.

I suddenly dropped the tin tray of pies. They crashed all over the tiled kitchen floor. Due to Aimee's screams of delight from the living room when she'd answered the phone.

"Oh, Daddy, Daddy … Is that really you, Daddy … Just let me get Mummy … Daddy … Daddy … are you still there?" Oh, Daddy!

5

STANLEY

It's two years since I've seen the lad. He seemed so settled at work, and all.

Anne tells me I'm making myself ill.

"Stanley, please love. You can't carry on like this. You don't sleep, you're smoking your head off and those days at the Legion aren't helping you know love, all that boozing."

I know she's only trying to help but it ain't her lad that's gone, A.W.O.L. I'm bleeding worried daft 'bout our Stan, it ain't like him. He's always been so sensible. The one everybody else could rely on. I don't know I just don't get it at all.

That summer of 2008 was such a relief, when a letter came in our post. I was so made up; I remember I'd been taking Midge on a walk on the common and me friend Anne was back at the house. She'd put my post for that day on the mantel piece, above the fireplace.

"Oh, Anne, love, Anne that's our Stan's hand writing on this post you know, I said, I could feel the weight of six months of worry falling from me, even before I ripped the envelope open.

But I was none the wiser really when I read his letter,

Dear Dad,

I'm sorry if you're in a state, over my whereabouts, but I'm safe and I'm just wanting to get me head together. Since we lost Mum and it didn't work out between me and Julia I've not been happy, to say the least Dad.

On top of this work had been stressing me out no end. Please don't worry I'm fine and I'll be back when I feel more able to think straight.

Take care Dad,

Love from

Stan x

"Bloody hell, Anne, love," I said once I'd read his letter a few times. "What the hell is the young fool playing at, Anne? I don't understand any of it. He knows he could have come to me. We always talked over any crap we were both going through. It's just a bloody mystery this lot, love. It is as well."

"Calm down, Stanley, love. Listen, where's the envelope?" Anne said as she rummaged in the fire place on her hands and knees. I had thrown this away. Desperate to know Stan was safe and well. But worried, discarding it.

Anne put the pieces of white oblong paper back as they had been. She placed the pieces before me on the dining room table.

"Look, Stan, look there, that's where he must be," she said, pointing.

I sparked up one of me roll ups and drew heavily on the fag, taking into my lungs a good strong dose of the harsh tobacco.

"What, Anne, my little love, am I looking at, may I ask?" I said smiling and lowering my head close to the shattered, screwed up envelope. I always acted daft when life got too much and I then put me specs on before looking even closer at the torn paper.

"Stop acting the goat, Mr Peel Senior" Anne said, which was usually a sign she was narked with me.

That night down on Clapham Common Anne made me feel so much better. We liked to go to the Legion. The place where we had met up again after all those years, just after we had both lost our loved ones.

The Legion was off the High Street in spitting distance of the Common. "Thanks Anne," I said when I'd sat down having been served with me pint of Guinness.

"What for, love?" she said, knowing very well what I was talking about.

"For pointing out the grubby post mark on our Stan's letter of course," I said smiling and losing some of me pint down the front of me new white shirt and waistcoat.

"Oh that, thought you'd never mention it," she replied.

We both laughed and had a good old time finishing off the night with a dance to a Glenn Miller tune, the resident band struck up with.

Just before Christmas of the first year that Stan disappeared, he wrote again. But this time there were no clues and he simply put,

Hi Dad,

I'm fine, Merry Xmas.

Your loving son, Stan x

The stamp had no postmark. No chance this time of tracing him. Not that Anne and I got anywhere with the Sheffield stamp on the first letter.

Anne went to Sheffield a couple of times that first year. She had lived there for a time when she had been married to her late husband.

"But it's changed ever so much, Stanley," she said sadly, on her return home.

"I couldn't remember half of the places me and our Jack knew. The house we lived in near the city centre. Well I remember that alright. But there's a Casino there now, love. Oh, Jack, I'm so sorry, love." Anne had been a trooper travelling up on the coach to Sheffield. She hadn't been well either, and I was feeling heavy hearted again when she returned. Not to mention guilty. I intended to travel with her. But I was advised by the Doc not to because my blood pressure was sky high. I was in poor physical health at the time.

By the autumn of the second year of Stan's leaving Anne bumped into an old friend of ours from our school days. Derek Miles, Anne and I had all grown up together in Clapham. Anne had left Clapham Road High School and became a dancer. She travelled all over Europe in the 1950s and 60s before returning to Sheffield when she met Jack.

They raised a family and it was many a year before Clapham called again.

As for me, I left school and worked at different jobs, including labouring and decorating all over London. On different building sites and other places. I set up my own little business in 1964, just before we had Stan. Kate and I ran a great little 60s coffee bar and store just up from the common.

Derek was a constant presence in Clapham from leaving school. He joined the Metropolitan Police, and was a very popular lad in the force, and with the public in South London. He became a sergeant, retiring with great acclaim from all who worked and he served in the force.

That cold, frosty fog drenched autumn afternoon Anne threw a stick in the park for our little Yorkshire terrier Midge. She went bounding after the little stick but didn't return for a long time. The fog was as thick as the old London smog of yesteryear. But after a while a tall, dapper old man came out of the mist. Just like some old film and it unnerved Anne. I was a little on edge myself. But once the pea souper of a mist lifted I knew who this lad was carrying our little Midge in his arms.

"Well blow me away. You old bugger, it must be ten years. No more, Derek. Well I never! It's our great

31

neighbourhood bobby, one Mr Derek James Miles as I live and breathe!"

Bumping into Derek changed everything. Anne and I told him all about our sleepless nights and intense worries over Stan.

Every time we all went to the Legion Derek was a massive help. Ever after that joy drenched, autumn day Derek met us in the club a couple of times a week.

By Christmas of 2009 Derek had some fantastic news. He had still got some strong friendships and contacts in the police force.

"I will certainly try to help all I can, Stanley, my old son," Derek had said when we renewed our friendship with him. By the 18th of December he was as good as his word.

By January of 2010 in the Legion Anne was to reassure me as ever. I sat near the stage, my pint of Guinness going stale. I was on edge more than usual.

"Come on, Stanley, love, Derek's been up in Sheffield a fortnight now; I'm sure when he rolls in here tonight he will have something positive to tell us." Anne squeezed my hand and smiled sweetly. She was a great girl.

Derek had said he would go up north for a few days and make some enquiries to our Stan's whereabouts. By 10.00 p.m. that night in the Legion I was so grateful to my friend.

Derek breezed into the Legion and sat down with his half pint of bitter. He made himself comfortable next to us.

"I've found out what has happened to Stan," he said.

6

EMILY

"I don't know what else to do Ruth; I've tried everything I can think of to find her. We both have ... oh ... I do ...n't ... know ... any ... more."

It was a week before Christmas. 2008 was to be with us sooner than we knew; Ruth, my best friend, had been great. They all had on the estate. The police, the homeless charities, everyone and even a clairvoyant that summer!

"Come on, Emily, darling, don't cry," Ruth said, holding my hand while she searched for a tissue.

"Here, babe, dry your eyes. We'll find her, it's 'cause it's Christmas love, it's cause it's when she left at this time of year I mean."

"I know ... I ... know," I said.

Ruth was right of course. Mum went missing the week before the Christmas, two years before! It's still raw and hard to take that time of year without Mum.

"Why don't we go into Glasgi' darling," Ruth said.

"Cheer us selfs up. Then go into Strachan's café on the way back?"

"See if Jack has any bright ideas 'bout what to do next?"

"Or anyone off the estate that might be just passing time in there?"

"Oh thanks, Ruth, you are so good to me! Everyone has been. I don't deserve it, I've been a nightmare through this."

"Yi know wi, Mum, I'd don't know … I really don't know?"

"Come on, Em', don't upset yourself anymore, get your glad rags on and let's get into town for the afternoon."

We left my flat, the one I shared with my Mum Jane, at about midday. The weather was foul. But Scottish weather is. No matter if you live in Edinburgh or Aberdeen or like us on the outskirts of Glasgow. The winters can be harsh and brutal. They take some battling through some years.

Ruth's suggestion though to cheer us both up, that day was a really good idea. We got to the bottom of where Mum had gone, finally, by teatime. Although I had mixed feelings at the news, my heart almost broke.

We caught the number 20 bus from outside. Jack Strachan's café and we were on the main street of Glasgi' city centre forty minutes later.

We had a right laugh and I forgot my constant worries, for those few hours at least.

Ruth had a thing about her; she absolutely loved to dress up. This always made her fantastic company.

That's how I met Ruth

I was working part time in town just before Mum disappeared. Jack at the café had a friend who ran a stall in the market, near the bus station in Glasgi'.

"Hi, Em'," he said one day, as he mopped up some spilt tea and mess in his café.

"God I'm glad today's over."

"I've had the Bash street kids in off the Monroe Estate. So I love 'em so I do! But the messy little mites, Em', you know."

I had been in Jack's café all afternoon that day. I think it had been near Guy Fawkes night I remember there were fireworks and more noise and fuss going on than usual, anyhow, I was not feeling like I could be bothered with anything. In fact, looking back I was very worried about me Mum then, I think she might have been thinking of taking off at that time, I don't know but that morning we had words. We had hardly ever argued, but Mum was being so odd, like a stranger really. She was preoccupied and seemed to have the worries of the world on her shoulders, I was a bit snappy and off with her and I ended up going to Jack's that afternoon.

"Jane Clay for gid's sake woman, what is it? Please tell me, shall we go out for the day? We are getting like stir crazy in this hovel of a flat," I remember saying when I couldn't stand Mum staying mute and distant all that morning.

"It's Mum to *yi*, young lady and jist yi remember that in future." she said, snappy like I hadn't known her ever before.

I left the flat then, there dint seem any point trying to reason wi' her. I was worried though all that afternoon in the café. I couldn't find my mobile phone, when I did decide to leave Mum be for a while, and I ended up slamming the front door of the flat which knocked off an ornament from its perch on a little table in the hallway. Mum shouted something after me, but I was so frustrated with her moods I dint go back to discover what she had to say I thought I'd leave her to 'cool down.'

"You ok, Em', love?" Jack asked when he'd locked the café up.

"No, Jack, I'm not happy today, not at all really. Oh I'll be fine I'm just fed up. Me and Mum had a bit of an argument that's all and I'm really fed up living around here some days."

Jack sorted out his till and put the day's takings in the safe in the back room. He then turned the red open and closed sign around to let folk know he had shut up shop.

He sat with me a while and I told him what had happened at home that morning.

"I know, lassy, I think it's when family spend too much time under the same roof, I'm same wi' me wife Jenny at weekends when I'm not in here. She says I get under her feet all the time, and we're at odds wi' each other sometimes." Jack said calmly and smiled kindly.

Jack was a good confidant as he was always looking out for his customers. He generally knew when they were out of sorts, or maybe needed a chat. He would usually just say like he had to me.

"You ok so and so," or "Everything fine and dandy," or something like this.

He didn't carry on his concern any further. After nearly half a century on the estate and ten of those years running the café people knew his ways were genuine, caring and he was one who was there with advise or help if need be.

"Listen, lass," he said after I'd told him a few of my woes, recent ones anyway.

"I've got a friend who's busy at the moment. Well she's a pal of the wife's to be true. She has a stall near the station. On the market, in town. She keeps 'askin mi' Mrs if she knows of anyone who might like to earn a 'wee' bit of extra cash, two or three days a week part time like."

Jack's little chat 'wi' me and the offer of some work and extra cash really helped.

I started on Mary's (that was Jack's wife's friend) stall the following week. Mary sold hats, scarfs, handbags and jewellery. She made everything herself, and the little business had begun to flourish after a few years of trading on the market.

After a couple of weeks Mary said would I like to work Saturdays as well as the odd afternoon I did when I first started. I was so pleased when she gave me the chance. I loved the little job. I enjoyed all the different characters I needed to deal with. The stall became busy and time flew by, especially on those Saturdays.

One weekend a dark haired glamorous looking lass asked me how much one of the hats we had for sale was.

"How much is the maroon hat with the rainbow feather darling please?" she asked, I had expected her to talk posh Scots like they do some of 'em that come from Edinburgh way, but her harsh Glasgow tone was a mirror of mine and Mum's.

So Ruth buying the flamboyant hat was the start of our friendship. We began to bond when she bought hats, scarfs and other luxuries from Mary's trendy stall. This led to us meeting up for coffee in Jack's café. Eventually Ruth would crash at my flat after we had nights out in Glasgow, when our funds stretched to it.

But a week shy of Christmas 2007 Jack and Ruth Styles kept me in the dark about Mum. I had a blazing row in Strachan's with them both. I was devastated.

7

JANE

Part 2

I was banging like crazy on *Street Saviours'* office door. Stan was a few yards away from me bleeding and gurgling. I was going out of my mind.

"Help for fucks sake, help me! Come on! Open this fucking door! Someone, please!"

Once the police had arrived and I was taken to the hospital I knew my life had changed all over again.

They put me on a general ward at first. Or so I've been told since then. But all I can remember is waking up on the psychiatric wing. My head was aching, my heart stunned and broken. I was an emotional wreck! Numb of feeling, lost, broken and knowing I had a long, hard journey back to happiness and full health.

For the next six months I would try to rebuild my shattered life. I was heavily medicated, my memory hazy and my body frail when the time came for me to be discharged.

I had apparently let the police and my nurse know about Emily. But by the early weeks of June 2010 I had no idea of who I was still. Never mind who I knew, who I had been or who loved me if anyone at all. I was absolutely petrified when Doctor Marshall told me I was ready to leave the Sheffield Northern Hospital.

Andrea Marshall was a lovely lady. She understood. But the NHS cuts, the lack of beds and trained psychiatric staff meant I was to try and lead as normal life as possible, whatever that came to mean, God knows!

Through the help of the Northern Hospital, Andrea, and the wonderful folk at *Street Saviour*, I was able to tell my daughter Emily I was so deeply sorry for all the shit I had caused her. I had the opportunity to try to tell her what I had done. Why I had left my sweet, loving daughter high and dry for the past two years.

I spent all morning one Sunday putting pen to paper. Springtime had arrived in Sheffield. Andrea was putting the final touches to my paperwork. This was to finalise a move into my own flat. I found a nice quiet corner of the *Street Saviour* dormitory. Finding privacy was far from easy. But Sundays were fine. I sat with my writing pad and envelopes, pen and cigarettes, comfortable on my single bed, scared, tearful and lost for words to write to my daughter Emily. Words I knew if I wasn't careful I would end our fragile relationship, before I had the chance to rebuild this all over again.

By 4.00 pm that Spring Sunday evening I re-read my contact with Emily.

Sunday March 24th 2010
To Em,
Dearest Emily,

I know sorry is not enough and I apologise by this letter. It probably still doesn't heal the pain I've caused you.

Five years is a very long time darling. I know, you must have been worried sick. I'm sorry; I know sorry can't change all the time that's passed, all those Christmas Days. Your birthdays and all the happy times we should have shared.

It's taken me all morning and most of this afternoon Em to pen this note to you.

The reasons I ran away were because of your Dad, I know we never mention him, but he came back to see me. It was on your 25th birthday darling the 5th November 2005.

What happened left me poorly love. Your Dad hurt me again; I know this won't make any sense, because we have never mentioned him. But oh love I just couldn't handle seeing your Dad every day I can't explain in this letter love, but one day I hope you will understand.

Em please love can you find in your kind heart a place to forgive your old Mum, Please Em.

I have written the address I am staying below. Also the phone number for this hostel I'm in at the moment, I will leave it up to you now love. Give yourself time; I am very poorly again though at the moment. Something dreadful happened to me just before Christmas last year. No fault of my own Em I promise you, but I'm being cared for by the Hospital here in Sheffield as well as a homeless hostel in the city centre.

Ok love I will leave it all up to you now. Please take lots and lots of care of yourself and I love you always.

Mum x

I wrote the *Street Saviour* address and contact phone number at the foot of my letter, and sobbed my heart out. I knew Emily would find my writing to her very strange, she would have expected me to have jumped on a train out of Sheffield Station over the border of our home near Glasgow.

But I wasn't well enough to get home to Paisley. I was too fragile and ill to face all Em's questions and those of the folk back home. But the real reason I wrote and didn't phone Emily was due to her Dad. Jack Strachan wanting to be a part of my life again; I just couldn't let Emily know who her father was. Jack was always so kind to my daughter. Emily knew nothing of Jack being her other parent.

In the letter I'd told our secret lie that I'd said her Dad had suddenly turned up again. But in reality he had seen his daughter everyday of her life.

8

STAN

I was feeling lost. Gary and Jane were nowhere to be found and I missed them.

Usually I would catch up with Jane on the seat outside the Cathedral. Gary usually caught up with us in another part of Sheffield most days.

But I hadn't heard, seen or knew anyone who had been in touch with them for weeks. By that bleak, freezing cold first week of November I'd made a decision.

I didn't know the date, not until I found an ageing copy of the *Street Saviour* for that week. The *Saviour* came out on a Friday, so on the 4th I walked up to the South Way. The South Way was a duel carriage way out of Sheffield, the road which a couple of miles later blended into the M1 Motorway; south to London.

I was pretty much frozen solid; my hands the worst numb as I'd ever known them and my feet were going the same way.

I was just about to give up on this game of hitching back South; when a navy blue van shuddered over from the mists and darkness of the night. God knows how he or she or anybody else could have spotted me!

They pulled over. The exhaust of the 1970's Minivan blowing hard, and other ominous sounds made me think "God Stan, this is a shit plan."

When I'm settled in with the driver a few minutes later, I catch a look at someone in the passenger door window. Christ I looked like death warmed up as my old mother used to say, if someone looked far from well.

My lank mousey brown hair was plastered to my scalp; rain drops drenching my already sodden parka coat. My chocolate eyes sunken into my skull. I looked as pale as a white sheet. I had no colour what so ever and I was numb. My whole body solid cold ice.

The lad who kindly gave me a lift was a giant of a man. I couldn't help but notice his knees were high up, almost squashed right under the steering wheel. I was no dwarf of a bloke, but this lad must have towered high above me. I didn't discover this though 'til we stopped at the services a couple of hours later.

The lad who I hitched with was called Shane. I don't suppose he would have been so cramped up over the steering wheel if it hadn't had been a Minivan. One of those which are quite roomy behind the front seats funnily enough, but not a car for such a long trek to my old home town of London.

Shane was a man of few words, pleasant enough, but the night was foul. Fog, rain, wind and freezing cold temperatures. I think old Shane didn't have the appetite for conversation. He needed all his concentration to get us both safely to the capital. I maybe think it was at the back of his mind that his beloved navy blue Mini was on its last legs. Or wheels!

I'd travelled before from Golders Green coach station, when I was doing fine at the accountants. The job I thought would see me through to retirement one day.

Golders Green is a quiet, easier place to catch a coach. There isn't the hustle and bustle and panic of a big London Station and it's not as intimidating as say Victoria or one of the huge London stations.

"Good luck, lad, hope everything works out. Oh and take this, I won't have thee starving yousen."

I was really touched by the way Shane said goodbye to me. He dropped me off near to the coach station, just by the side of a park. Not so much a park really, more of a kid's playground. There were swings and a slide. But I was grateful most of all for the covered seating.

Shane climbed back into his van, waving out of the window as he chugged out of Golders Green. I gripped the £20 note he'd kindly given me, and was thankful there were folk who still cared.

I'd come to feel real affection for the people of Sheffield. I'd only been thrown into the city by misfortune, but once I'd mastered the accent, of being able to work out how they spoke I became really fond of the city. Shane's was the broadest I'd heard. I'd noticed a Barnsley Football Club sticker on his windscreen, so I thought maybe the Barnsley accent was even harsher, and a little tougher to pick up in a way.

I crashed on the bench under the covered seating of the playground.

I didn't have the faintest idea of the time, not since Shane had dropped me off. That was 2.00 ish in the morning, but I'd slept like crap when my head hit the hard, tough bench surface.

My sleep was lousy. I hadn't had a decent restful night since I'd hit Sheffield Station. That was over two years ago now. I must have slept soundly at some point in that time, but I couldn't think when. Bloody lack of kip can send a lad crackers!

I lit a fag when I stirred from another dose of broken sleep. Darkness still dominated Golders Green. I reckoned dawn was still well and truly a stranger to the town.

I rummaged in my damp, black holdall for my fags, sat up on my playground seat and rolled the cigarette paper tightly around the tobacco. I put in a filter and drew heavily on this; the nicotine a comfort to my sore hot throat and a joy to my aching body and legs.

I rummaged in my khaki parka coat pockets where I'd got change from sales of the *Street Saviour* over the past few days. In fact I began to feel delight for once. The note, coins and silver I found in my coat along with the few quid Shane had gifted me made me feel like a rich man. Relatively speaking of course. I had wonderful chills of joy falling through my spine; I then chuckled out loud to myself on the bench. This led to me bursting into hilarious laughter. I was exhausted, lost and amazed at where my life had ended up. But I just suddenly couldn't help myself. The joy a pittance of money in my old khaki parka could bring me was so ironic. I laughed myself to sleep.

God knows how long I had been dead to the world, or to Golders Green. But I was woken to the most enjoyable sight. The sun had come shining through the park, warming my sodden body as I lay under the covered seat. Laughter and sounds of joy filled the air. Children and parents were enjoying the glorious winter sunshine.

"You ok, Mr, my Mummy said to ask if you ok, Mr?"

I rubbed my sleep clogged eyes as I searched in my holdall for my broken specs. No joy, so I rubbed my eyes more. My vision was all blurs and distorted images.

"Mummy, I'm scared!"

I could hear perfectly well, the frightened child's voice, making me feel anxious. I began to panic.

When my vision cleared along with my head from heavy, prolonged sleep I sat upright.

By teatime I had once again received kindness from strangers. I'd woken on the playground bench at lunch time that day. Preschool children and their parents loved Golders Green Park so this was the scene my weary body encountered.

The little girl and her Mum who were so concerned about me were called Marie and Sophie. Marie ran back to her friends and I sat on the swings. Sophie was kind. She asked if I was feeling poorly and told me later in a café nearby that she and her hubby Trevor thought I might have died.

"You looked like a ghost, mate!" Trevor said at teatime that day.

"I, Sophie and Marie were really concerned. You've got some blood and colour back now though, son. Ain't' he, love?"

"Oh thanks to you all I must say I've been a lot livelier in my time. Thanks again." This made all the parents and kids in the cafe chuckle. I wasn't aware I'd cracked a joke, but I must have.

The café was called 'Good as Gold'. The playground had been built by the parents. They had raised money to help the kids of the area. They then had enough cash to build the cosy, friendly little café by the side of my bedroom, the covered seating which I used the night before.

That night I was going to try and visit my old Dad. This had been my intention when I hitched from the South Way back in Sheffield. But I couldn't face thinking about how to. I wish to God I had gone back home. I made the biggest damn mistake of my whole life that night I hitched another lift back to Sheffield, a fatal mistake!

9

STANLEY

Derek looked terrible; his face ashen and grey. I knew he had something grim to tell us, I just knew!

"Bloody hell fire, Anne!" I said as I made for the Legion bar. This was the first week of January and that Sunday night was dead quiet. 2009 had been celebrated in style in the club. I asked Anne if she minded having a quiet night at home. I didn't feel up to a jolly New Year's Eve song and dance. Stan was still playing on my mind. The two years he had been absent from our lives had left my heart saddened. My appetite for life lessened by my lad's disappearance.

Anne made old Derek comfortable. She moved a couple of chairs away from the table we were drinking at. He fell with relief on to the comfort of the wine coloured seating. Seating which ran the length of the concert room in the Legion Club.

I placed a pint of bitter and a double brandy in front of him. His cheeks blossomed rosy again and our good old Derek Miles resurrected himself before us.

"Bloody hell fire, Del, lad, you o ... you ... you ok, Del?" I said feeling out of sorts myself all of a sudden.

"I'm worried about the pair of you now, Stanley, are you ok? You look a bit peaky to me; you can hardly get your words out, love!"

I thanked Anne, closing my hand over hers as Derek removed his grey, rain sodden coat; one which always reminded me of the 1960s. One of the knee length rain coats that were popular back then.

Derek had one gentle gulp from his brandy, but couldn't contain himself. He wretched and was violently sick, knocking over the contents of our table. I helped Anne loosen my good friend's tie, as she held him up before he fell from the seating, ending up in a heap on the Legion's claret, sickly carpet.

Once we had come to terms with what had happened another year had sped by. Derek had to give alcohol and ciggies a miss after that night he came home from Sheffield. After the fright he gave us all in the club.

Derek had never married or dated many women really. He always gave his life to the police force; content to work long hours. He loved the variety and friendship his vocation provided. So when he retired, he was so very pleased to help us. He was delighted when Anne and I asked him about Stan. There had been a time when Stan had been interested in joining the police as a teenager. Derek had given the lad his advice. Stan always looked on Del as the Uncle he'd never known. He was an only child, and with Derek not having been blessed with children, this was fine for them both. Derek thought a lot of our Stan throughout his life.

Once we had buried Stan, on what was the most heart-breaking day of my life, I had a long chat with everyone.

I asked the Legion's staff if they would put on a few snacks. They obliged with sandwiches and such like. Only myself, Anne, Derek, and Julia were at Stan's wake. I did ask young Jane, who had been kind enough to attend but she had to decline. Jane had lived rough in Sheffield, becoming very fond of our Stan, they helped each other out a lot.

"We became very good friends you know, Mr Peel, he was a lovely lad, I'm so terribly sorry," Jane told me.

I could plainly see the girl was distraught over my lad; I was very grateful and so touched by her words. Julia and Anne made sure she was looked after. They made certain she caught her train back to Sheffield on time. Her nurse Andrea who attended the service with her thanked us all for our care and kindness to Jane.

"I remember when I first met Stan; he was so shy and unsure of himself. I'll miss him so much," Julia said sipping her bloody Mary drink at the Legion bar.

The steward Ray had given the place over to us for the afternoon. We had lost our Stan on Christmas Eve. So not until a fortnight or so into 2009 were we able to say our goodbyes to him. For the funeral, a quiet affair, I'd asked Reverend Paul, our local vicar to organise everything. The local church of St. Matthew's in Clapham had brought great solace to us all. The day was thankfully kind as far as the weather went, sunny, chilly but pleasant.

Julia, Anne, Derek, myself and Ray sat on stools at the Legion bar. We put a few quid in the Juke box; Julia selected some of my lad's songs. Records we all knew he loved. Music was very important to Stan. He drove his Mother to distraction with his racket when he lived at home. As a teenager Kate would often cut the electric in the house, pulling the main switch as a last resort to get Stan to tone down his noise.

"Oh God he drove us around the twist with this tune, Julia, love, Oh I wish I hadn't been so hard on ... on ... the ... lad," I said as Julia selected the record Stan adored all his life.

"You were always there for him, Mr, don't blame yourself, love," Julia added wiping away a heavy tear from her cheek. Mascara began to stain her face, as more tears came. Tears of pain but then of joy, as we remembered how much joy Stan had brought us in his short, daft life.

Raymond had been a good mate of Stan's. They had hooked up when they started High School in the 1980's. So it was apt that Ray should be there to run the bar that day.

"Oh, dear, he adored The Pogues and this song, Mr Peel" Ray said. I laughed out loud all of a sudden.

"What's tickling you then, Mr Stanley Peel?" Anne asked, as I nearly went flying from my high stool at the bar on to the Legion's claret carpet.

"It's Ray, I've known the lad most of his days, and he still calls me Mr ... oh ... Mr," I had another fit of giggles "Mr Peel ... oh ah, ah."

"Raymondo!" I said as 'Rainy Night in Soho', the beautiful song Stan loved, came to a close on the juke box.

"Yes, Mr Peel, Sir!" He said, but now I knew he was having me on!"

He winked at me, mischievous as ever.

We all had more drinks that afternoon than were maybe good for us. But Stan's favourite tunes, Julia, Derek and Anne's memories and the banter between me and Ray made for a wonderful send off to the lad. The funeral and wake was a real, tender comfort to me, to Julia and the others.

By around 7.00 pm that night we sang along to "Rainy Night in Soho," for the very last time. Raising our chosen drinks to my loving son Stanley James Peel.

"God Bless You Stan Lad" we all cried out as the Pogues faded to the crackles of the vinyl record, on the old juke box in the corner.

10

EMILY

I walked into an atmosphere I could have cut with a knife. I mean Jack and Ruth were as thick as thieves in the cafe, just shy of Christmas that year.

I had been helping out on Mary's market stall. I'd been set on at spring time. The stall was really great for me, taking my mind off Mum's whereabouts, and so easing my debts. Debts which had been mounting up, as I had to stand for the rent. Mum and I could just about manage. But since she'd left I was finding life a little bit tough.

By the autumn of 2009 Ruth began to be a wee bit of a stranger. We didn't go out, hardly at all and I was being told by folk she and Jack in the café were becoming more than chummy. She rarely called to buy anything at the stall anymore, or just pop by the flat for a catch up or a cuppa. I missed her; I rarely took any of the estate tittle-tattle and gossip seriously. Too many folk on the Monroe had little else to entertain them. What they dint know at times they liked to create or make up, not all of the time, but now and again.

But the rumour chain of gossip had been true this particular time!

I'd been working on Mary's stall all that day. Christmas trade had been brisk. I loved the job, but as I jumped off the bus I began to feel the exhaustion. My limbs sagged and my head throbbed. The pain of a stressful Saturday had shown itself all too well. I dropped in at Strach's to revive myself. I wish to God I'd just walked on a little further though. I strode the few hundred yards to the sanctuary of my flat.

All was quiet as I stepped over the threshold of Strach's café; the lights subdued and the tables set for the next week's customers. Jack and Ruth were hidden away. Two silhouette figures sat over a flickering candle light. Only the chequered red and white table cloth lit up in the blackness. Their loving laughter and chat ceasing as soon as I entered the solitary chime of the door's bell echoed. For such a tiny bell, which told Jack he had customers, she made a real impression.

I had never in all my twenty-five tender years been so overcome with anxiety. The place oozed secrets; the atmosphere tense and uneasy.

Jack came out of his chair, scraping the legs on the tiled floor.

"Oh it's E ... Em ... Emily!" he said.

I knew when he said this something wasn't as it should be. Not in all the days and years I'd known Jack Strachan had he called me Emily. Jack had been a presence in my life as far back as I can remember. The way he was acting, stiffening and blushing red, all told me something at Strach's that night was amiss.

Ruth was pissed! When we had first met she never drank a drop of the stuff. She only tended to have tea or mineral water. By October time she had changed so much. Liaisons with different shady blokes, being unreliable, and the booze, well the bottles of wine. I didn't 'git' her any more.

"Don't, Jack, love," I said quietly "I've had a tough day on the stall. I just need to have five minutes and I'm off to mi bed."

Then Ruth pissed me off more than ever my old ma' could do at times.

"Oh bloody hard day on yi … hic, hic … up … pff … oh it's i piece oh … hic … cake, Emily, dar … li …in … hard day my arse!"

I totally ignored her; I'd seen her in that poxy drunken state before and I knew not to react. I was fuming. My head was ready to burst with the stress of everything.

But when I noticed the letter I gave it them both! They got all the pent up shite, anger, fury and injustice of me and mine!

Jack took the bottle of Merlot wine from the table, along with an overflowing glass before Ruth. He then pulled her from her seat. Not with any malice, but with enough persuasion to let her know she'd had enough, and that he was on my side after all.

By the time her taxi had pulled up outside mine and Ruth Styles, a once glowing friendship had collapsed.

As Jack held Ruth upright by the flickering broken street lights on Monroe Street, I read the letter. A letter that was laid bare on the café table. The table Jack and

Ruth had just parted from. A letter which I just couldn't fathom; one I was angry again over. One I was weeping like a bairn over. A letter of betrayal!

I just couldn't believe it of Jack. I stormed out of his café, screwing up the letter tight.

"You bastard!" I said for all the 'Monroe' to know about.

"And you! You nasty little posh Scottish slut!" I may as well have not bothered insulting 'Miss up your own arse Styles', 'cause she was out of it. Seated, or slumped in the doorway of Strach's, oblivious to my temper and disgust.

When I got back to my flat I re-read the letter from Mum. A letter Jack had for the past month or so, dated 15ᵗʰ November 2009.

Dear Jack,

Darling I miss you so much, I had to get away from you, I'm so very sorry my love. I've always loved you and because recently I have wanted you so badly again, I couldn't stand not telling Em' about you.

I had it all worked out to tell our Emily about you Jack, but I panicked. The debts were doin' my head in. Xmas was creeping upon me, I thought Emily was never going to find a decent job, and I'd fallen for you Jack darling all over again.

The letter Mum had written to Jack was long. I fell into a deep long and dreamless sleep, having only read the first couple of paragraphs.

But my blissful slumber didn't make waking up the next day easy. In fact, I wished myself millions of miles away from the Monroe, Glasgow city and that poxy little flat I called home!

11

CHARLOTTE

Once Christmas Eve, Christmas Day and the following day had come and gone I was a wreck.

Gary's bolt out of the blue phone call triggered upheaval. Both Aimee and that Christmas were hell for me.

Once I'd cleared away the chaos that was my little kitchen, throwing away all the food and cleaning up the wreckage of my home, I sat and wept again. Aimee was in tears. She clung to the telephone in the living room. I couldn't trace the number, Gary had phoned from the number withheld.

"Oh, Aimee, darling, please, come on sweetheart, give me the phone I don't think it was Daddy at all. I think it was Uncle Roy acting daft. You know how silly he is sometimes? He has a silly sense of humour you know he does, Uncle Roy you know!"

"Mummy, it was Daddy, he will phone back I know he will."

Aimee's screams were new ones. She hollered and screeched at the top of her lungs, her beautiful pale face red, with tears flooding from her. She pulled at her gorgeous fair hair and I was lost. I was in shock at her reaction and I was fuming with Gary. Despite my little joke that I'd told Aimee, I was pretty certain Gary had phoned I'd picked up calls before in the past three years, calls that unnerved me, calls that were withheld, ones which were around Christmas time or near to Aimee's birthday, around August 1st.

By the time 2.00 am Christmas morning arrived I was exhausted. My nerves were raw. As I sat in the solitude and silence of the living room I tried to make sense of everything.

I caught a glance of myself; the television showed me how I was. My reflection one of exhaustion; my long fair locks greasy and unkempt. I took out my compact mirror for a more realistic look - I looked ten years older than my 43. I had dark course circles under my eyes. A bewildered lady I didn't know anymore.

Only the constant reminders of Santa Clause found Aimee fighting sleep. She dropped the phone. Hours after Gary's mindless call, I carried her upstairs, putting her safely into our bed. She hadn't slept in our double bed for a very long time. But I'd had to keep her content to be there if she suddenly woke, or had a bad dream again. These dreams had subsided, but it was as if Gary had put us back a hell of a long way that Christmas Eve.

Christmas Day that year was a very subdued affair. I'd already asked Roy and his latest flame. I'd phoned him while Aimee still slept around 8.00 am.

"Roy, listen, love, I think Gary called again, last night," I said.

"Oh great, sis, when will he be ready to go down the club again love?"

I loved my kid brother, but he had two infuriating habits. I wasn't the only person he knew who couldn't abide the way he would interrupt you so rudely. But I think I was on my own in being hacked off with the way he trivialised everything, making jokes from even the most grave of situations.

"Don't be soft, Roy, and stop bloody interrupting me! You've done that ever since we were little and it's bloody rude you know!"

I couldn't help love Roy though. If he was ever told of his failings he was a sweetheart. He'd be guaranteed to annoy the hell out of you again. But he'd apologise forever. Then he would come around and help out with any chores and be a cool loving brother to make up for it all.

"So, Charlotte, love, you want me to tell Aimes," when he called her 'Aimes' he was annoying as well.

"To tell Aimes that if she asks if I called pretending to be Gaz last night, to play along and say it was yours truly?" Roy was worried too. He always put a front on with folk. But when he asked me this, his voice wasn't calm, he wasn't kidding anymore. Roy and Gary were close, this was ever since I'd introduced them to each other when I'd first started dating Gary.

"No problem, Charlotte. No joking now, love, are you sure you're ok?"

That was Roy; he could upset the very hell out of you one minute and be as kind, sensitive and loving as an angel the next.

We all did our best for Aimee's sake. Roy and his girlfriend Lilly helped with the turkey and trimmings. We all mucked in. Roy and Lilly tried hard to entertain Aimee. But I seemed to spend most of the day nursing her on the sofa. She hardly played with her presents, she kept drifting into a deep sleep. She was shattered poor kid. Lilly was not at all shy. She was lively and the only person who made Aimee's face light up, by the time the Queen had finished her annual speech on the TV.

There was only 18 months in age between myself and Roy, but he always attracted young lasses. I don't think he'd dated anyone over 25 in all his dating career.

By the time darkness had made her arrival, and we had all flopped out on the big red sofa and comfy chairs in the room, Christmas that year had said farewell.

I was so pleased Lilly had come along though. By the time she came to leave the next day Aimee was more herself. She and Lilly were like sisters out in our back garden.

Snow had fallen overnight and they had a ball constructing a huge snowman, taking Roy's best leather jacket from the cloakroom and his daft Sheffield United Benny hat. Clothes for 'Snowy', the name Aimee chose to christen their creation.

When Roy suddenly caught on that Snowy was a finely dressed Snowman he ran out to frolic in the garden. A snowball fight and fun, laughter, and joy filled the air. I joined them, taking precious photos on my new phone; one Roy and Lilly had kindly gifted to me that day.

Aimee was a little tearful when Lilly left with Roy. But she was so delighted to have made a new friend.

Roy moved onto one more young lass some weeks later. But Aimee had made a true friend and so had I.

On Boxing Day afternoon I decided to take Aimee into the city centre. We hadn't left the house for days.

We needed a change of scenery. The snows had been brief. No sooner had there been a heavy flurry overnight, than the thaw came by midday. By around 2.00 pm that day the sun helped to cheer the city's chilly skyline. But Aimee had a further set back when she noticed the figure slumped on the big seat as we stepped off our bus.

Aimee had been great on the short journey into town. The number 67 bus was ideal, leaving from the end of our street. Once we had walked through the wooded path, having left home from our cul-de-sac avenue on the estate. Then Aimee always tried to press the silver button which made the little green man light up, making us safe to cross over to the stop on the other side of the main Sheffield Road.

She loved to take my hand and skip joyfully over to the shelter. That morning she was content. Her joyful time spent with Lilly had made her my beautiful Aimee all over again. She was carefree, quiet and only questioned anything she really didn't understand. Or ask me if I was feeling happy. I loved the way she had the habit of doing this.

"Mummy, are you happy today? If not, Mummy, then I am going to make you be happy," she said as she ran over to the fold down seat of the bus shelter.

My heart was at ease when she asked me this. Not since Gary had gone had she really been so free and easy about life. I was so relieved. My peace of mind returning, knowing I had my five-year-old darling back to her true self.

But when she recognised Gary straight away, as I did with absolute shock and panic, our Boxing Day slipped again. Our emotions sent spiralling into confusion and fear. Fear of the unknown!

I'd noticed him before Aimee had.

"Thank you, driver," I said as we stepped from the number 67.

"Say thank you, darling," reminding Aimee to do the same.

"Oh yeah, sorry, Mr, thanks, Mr," she said happy once again.

"Oreight, love, you're welcome," the driver said, his broad accent had Aimee chuckling. She always thought her Daddy was fun when he used to speak the same. Gary didn't have such a distinct Sheffield accent. But sometimes his dialect would surface and he would say something that meant he was from the city and nowhere else in the country.

"Oreight … oreight …!" Aimee said, playfully imitating the accent. But I gently reminded her not to do this.

"Ok, Aimee, love, don't it's not nice," I'd said smiling at her and taking her tiny hand. Before heading to take a shortcut, we were going to browse the shops on the main precinct, which always meant cutting through the gennel that led past the Cathedral. The big church in town had just been given a facelift and looked beautiful. Christmas lights adorned the tree next to the seating near her entrance.

Gary looked dreadful; he was caressing a can of strong lager. At one time, Roy had been drinking heavily, more than was good for him. He had lost his job, and things were difficult, so I recognised the Special Hops lager Gary held from those days when my kid brother drank the same stuff to excess.

I tried to steer Aimee in the opposite direction. Not taking her past the seats, but past the chain of shops that would take us down by the market. My mind was in flux.

Hoping Aimee hadn't seen her Dad, hoping I could work out what to do once we had made our way to the markets instead of the precinct.

Freeing herself from holding my hand, Aimee dashed across to Gary. A young woman was sat beside him, a pretty lass. Her hair was raven black, long yet very unkempt. She was deathly pale with reddish circles beneath her hazel eyes. Before Aimee fell into her father's lap, the woman was gone. As if she had been under a magic spell, she picked up a bottle of cider or wine. It was difficult to know, and simply disappeared.

"Daddy, Daddy, wake up please wake up. I love you Daddy. Look, Mummy, it's Daddy, look!" Aimee cried out as she threw her tiny arms around him. Gripping Gary tightly and then smothering him with an array of loving kisses.

I stood frozen, like a statue, in the cold; the temperature had dropped when we arrived in town. Snow had slowly begun to cover the ground, and I was lost stood staring in horror at Aimee and Gary. My mind a block of ice, or that's how it seemed. I couldn't think, I couldn't move, as though I was in a film. Some surreal movie or a dream, I hoped I was soon to wake from. And upon waking I would then be relieved to discover Aimee was fine and safe after all.

But this was real. Boxing Day teatime in the centre of Sheffield. Darkness had begun to arrive. The crowded city alive and joyful. Everyone was still savouring their holidays.

I came to my senses. Suddenly my stupid mind cleared. I took my heavy daft Russian effect hat off; I straightened my mousy fair hair and slipped off my crimson red fleece gloves.

"Amy, darling, let go please! Look my darling, you just sit there a little while, and relax. Just relax, love, Ok?"

Aimee flopped across to the corner of the seat; I held her hand as I sat calmly between my two loved ones.

I wasn't a hundred per cent sure about Gary; I still had my doubts about the man sat beside me being my husband of the past 24 years at all.

Boxing Day 2009 ended at the hospital. I sat with Aimee in a South Yorkshire ambulance, as we wondered if Gary was going to recover, wondering if his collapsing from the Cathedral seat was serious.

The 27th December was spent at my husband's bedside. Once he had been discharged from intensive care. Aimee constantly thanked the doctors and nurses of the Sheffield Northern Royal Hospital for their care. I was an emotional wreck by midnight that day.

12

GARY

I prefer the cell to being in the TV common room. That's what I call the place. I get paranoid with the rest of 'em. I prefer me own company, always have.

The summer's nearly over. This year has been shocking. I thought 2007, 2008, and last year were the hardest of my life. But no, ending up in here has really hit me hard. I miss Aimee most of all. Charlotte comes every week with her, but I'm ashamed, ashamed my only loving daughter has to travel all that way to see me in this shit hole of a place.

Every couple of weeks in here I see someone who helps me make sense of everything. She's a probation person in the nick in a way. All the prisoners need to see one. She helps some weeks, but does my head in others, if I can't face raking up all the shite that's gone before; I don't say 'owt or hardly 'owt anyway.

"So, Gary, thanks for agreeing to do this. So, Gary, tell me where it all went wrong, love?"

That's what she asked first time I went to see her. She was a young lass. She talked to me like I wa' a kid. That first time she did anyhow I remember thinking.

"For fuck sake, love, am I helping me sen or 'helpin' you?"! Once she'd patronised me for the first three or four times I saw her.

But she had a look of Charlotte and I found it helped after a couple of months. I didn't let on though. I still faked a cocky attitude. A 'I'm bloody bored of this shite' kind of thing. Not answering her half o' the time, sitting all cool, like a spoilt kid. Slumped in the chair, fiddling wi' me roll ups tin or staring through the window behind her.

She wa' cute though, about 20 odd, mousy fine hair, striking pale blue eyes and shy! She'd never hold my attention. I didn't feel reight looking at folk when I spoke to 'em. So Petra Steel counselled me. Like I say some weeks with success, others not.

I told her everything about when I'd left for work that morning, that Christmas of 2007. Of how I'd rarely been turning up at work, of lying to my customers, making excuses, shirking my decorating. So by a couple of weeks' shy of Christmas the lies and truth had become blurred. Deceit leaving me forgetful of who I had lied to and been straight with.

I remember the Friday everything finally fell apart. I dropped Aimee at school before driving into town and I parked the van down by the canal. I'd plenty of work in some of the flats over the years. I'd park up outside Gerry's place. He was an old pal. The flats overlooked the canal. He also had a house boat moored there. But Gerry was having a rough patch. When I hooked up with him again a few months after he'd left his wife, well, Sally and Gerry weren't actually married, but they had been as good as. Childhood sweethearts and living in each other's pockets for 20 odd years had been the same as being wed. Sally had left him, taking their teenage daughter Carla with her. She had always craved to live back in London, and Gerry was left lost, angry and in need of a mate to console him. But we were bad news for each other. At first we were like teenagers all over again. Jumping from boozer to boozer, bookies to bookies, we started to watch United play again. But we both began to play with fire. He'd always charmed the lasses and I got myself lost. I ended up cheating on Charlotte, when all our married life, I'd never as much as glanced at anyone else. I ruined our 15 years of marriage in just a few months, that summer and autumn of 2007. But the lead up to Xmas I'd been as bad for Gerry as he to me. Trying to relive past glories. Trying to turn back the hands of old father time. For a time we thought had been fantastic. In reality though problems came and went back in the mid-eighties for myself and Gerry. The same as they did when we hooked up once more in the 2000s.

That Friday shy of Christmas Gerry said, "Gaz I'm gonna tart up old Clarissa, why don't you give us a hand?"

I didn't have the faintest idea what he wa' on about, but by teatime that Friday his pride and joy Clarissa was looking as good as new. She was moored down on the canal. The Victorian quays had been derelict for years. But by the millennium Sheffield had been given a face lift. The canals had been reborn. Flats, off-licences, cafes sprung up overlooking the keys, Clarissa, Gerry's pride and joy houseboat, was reborn. She was transformed back into his floating treasure, I helped and in hindsight wish to God I'd left him to it. Left Gerry to get over Sally and Carla in peace. Wishing I'd finished old Mrs Spooner's decorating like I'd promised Charlotte I would. But we can all glance back and say 'I wish I'd …' or 'what if' or … I 'shudda done that' instead of this. Agreeing to tart up Gerry's houseboat that day was a big mistake for both of us, looking back.

For the next couple of months we were a bad influence on each other. Just like wayward teenagers. Rebelling against the world and the unfairness of our lives. As we both thought of them.

In reality we were trying to live out our youth. Trying to ignore that we had fucked up. Both of us throwing away loving relationships, our family, and bright futures.

Gerry had been a success. Growing up on the same estate; we'd been mates since being kids. He lived a few doors away from Sally Miles. They were inseparable from being in their early teens. Sally's parents and family were Londoners. She often went back with Gerry spending months and holiday times in Camden Town. Sally's Mum was a very vivacious talented singer, and touring the capital with various bands over the years. Often Sally would accompany her on tour. Gerry and Sal's Dad would support the bands, driving the equipment of drums, guitars, amplifiers and crew to the gigs.

Charlotte and Sally were very good friends. Juggling with my footballing career, I sometimes joined the adventures to London with them all. Times were, if United were away in or around Camden, north, south or the outskirts of London town, I would still play for us. Then hook up with Gerry, Charlotte, Sally and the gang at whichever venue they were to play. Heady days, times of great discovery of us all!

As the 1980s diminished and the 1990s sped by Gerry and Sally became a success. Sally had a lot of her Mum's musical traits. A beautiful singing voice and an accomplished piano player. Gerry had always aspired to write. Back in our school days he was always streets ahead of us all with English and Art. He wrote and illustrated horror books and short novels which were a big hit with teenagers and folk in their early twenties. Sally's Mum Sheena gave her the house she had grown up in. The Sheffield semi-detached where she had been raised, toddled around with Gerry and they had grown up. Grown up to become exceptional people.

So Gerry and Sally tended to flit between Sheffield and Camden. They bought a beautiful Georgian house near Camden Lock. Renovated this and had some amazing parties.

Heady times for us all. I kept in close touch with Gerry up until Charlotte told me about Aimee in 2002. The news I was to be a father at 39. Amazed, worried, and proud I drifted away from Gerry and Sally. Our friendship became a casual and less intense one, seeing each other still but usually only every few months as opposed to every day or week.

Charlotte had more regular contact with Sally, but that was something I rarely kept up to date with.

By teatime that Friday we had made Clarissa the houseboat look like a new penny, shiny inside and out. She looked lovely.

"Come on, Gaz, lad, let's get us sens off up to The Lion, then up the North end of town boozers. It's gonna be just like the old days, you and me against this big bad world. Or shit town, Sheffield any road!"

Gerry said, necking another can of lager.

"Slow down, you silly sod. We've got all neight, ya always bloody rushing about, Gez!" I said.

I was up for a fine old crawl around the old watering hole haunts of town as much as Gerry, even though they had mostly all changed, by name, staff and atmosphere. But I had always been the sensible cool headed one. I knew from those past halcyon days (which were rarely ever that, looking back really) that my old pal could be reckless. Reckless with his money, his health and most of all his lifestyle.

"Oh bloody hell 'old mother hen' strikes again," Gerry said, jumping from the houseboat on to the canal tow path. Gerry's appearance had changed little over the years. Lanky, blonde crew cut hair and thin as a stick of skeggy rock. But the deep lines and crow's feet under his eyes were evidence of a past. One in which he'd been 'Jack the Lad' more than was any good for him at times. He also put on the front of being the jester. But he was a worrier. So he couldn't kid on to me he was 'happy Larry' any more than anyone else who cared for him.

We walked and 'larked about, locking up Clarissa and crossing over the busy main road to the markets, having totally ignored the hectic traffic, by sprinting over the crossing, which met us as we left the canal keys. The Steelers Rest was a real flea pit of a pub. At one time known for all and sundry getting in there. Mainly the folk who worked on the markets, but also a place popular with any soul who was either on their way to the courthouse, or relieved they had been pardoned a taste of sometime at Her Majesty's Pleasure. The Steelers was one of only a handful of boozers in our city that hadn't changed that much, either by name, customers or otherwise over the years.

The Steelers pub was lifeless. I ordered a couple of pints of lager, glanced at the clock behind the bar and looked for Gerry. He'd made himself at home by the jukebox. Neither of us had been in there for well over five years, maybe more. An old lad sat at the bar, nursing a half pint of stout. A thin, unkempt character wearing a pork pie hat and moth eaten United shirt, jeans and holey trainers which had seen much better days. He fed peanuts to his sleepy Yorkshire terrier, mumbling to himself, not noticing we'd walked in at all at six o clock.

The cobwebs, old Christmas decorations and nicotine stained appearance told us the place had been neglected.

"This lager tastes like piss, Gaz. Come on, this place was always a bloody dive. Let's go to the Lion, lad. We had hardly touched our pints before heading off towards the bus station. I wasn't a fan of the Red Lion, but Gerry was. He still popped in some lunchtimes and the odd evening to see who was in. I hadn't been in any of the city centre boozers since well before we'd had Aimee. A good ten years I would say. I never thought owt of the Red Lion. A pub set in the heart of the bus and railway station. Not a seedy place, but I was never at ease in there, never comfortable with the place.

While Gerry mingled with some of the regulars in The Lion, I gulped down a good half of my pint, and put a couple of quid in the quiz machine near the gents, and hoped Gerry didn't want to spend hours in there.

I won my money back on the machine, then turned to check that Gerry still had most of his pint left. I needn't have worried.

"Come on, Mr Childs, old boy, we're off, sup up!" Gerry said, gently patting me on the back. I was relieved, but I knew something had happened. Swift exits from favourite boozers for Gerry usually meant he'd crossed someone, or said something. I knew him of old well enough to just 'sup up' and hear about it on the way to the next boozer, or at some point on our night out.

We walked across the road which was lined with bus stops. Up through the grotty, stinking underpass, which you rarely came through without encountering a homeless lad or lass. Gerry was silent all the way to the Golden Time. Summat was up, I knew Gerry, something was definitely up.

By the time we had had two pints and two Southern Comfort double chasers in the 'Golden Time' Gerry was distraught.

We only spent about half an hour in there. But in that time Gerry got barred for life, as did I. He had nearly assaulted the landlord and upset one of the student barmaids, bringing on great distress and nearly causing a bar room brawl. His silence from our short walk from The Lion had only been broken when he told the middle aged landlord: "Go fuck your mother up the arse every day you bastard!"

The landlord then had a couple of his heftily built bar staff drag Gerry on to the steps of the pub, and then threw him firmly into the road.

"Don't come back in here again, kid," he told me.

"I don't know what your problems are, I don't wanna know, but don't darken my pub doorstep again. Now fuck off home and sort yourselves out."

I picked Gerry up. He had smashed his head open on the kerb and was finding walking painful. I carried him across the road; sitting him down on the broad steps of the city library.

I managed to stem the heavy blood flow from his head wound with my tartan jacket, and inspected his knee through his ripped and bloody jeans.

Gerry passed out on the library steps a few minutes later. Blood flowing like a water fall from his head. His pallid features and white t shirt now red, saturated with his own blood, I called 999.

Over the weekend Gerry was admitted to the Royal Northern Hospital in Sheffield. He didn't get discharged for a fortnight. We calmed down for a while; living quietly on the houseboat. I did learn eventually why Gerry had nearly destroyed himself and the Golden Time that night. He had seen his daughter with an old flame of Sally's. Mick Waller and Gerry had never got on. They had toured around London with Sally, once her music had taken off. Mick was a talented guitarist. He flitted between being a session musician and helped out various bands, including Sally's 'Tearful Sunset', the band originally formed by her mum, Sheena.

A few weeks after the Golden Time pub debacle while we were relaxing on Clarissa, Gerry put a Nick Drake CD on and told me all about how Sally had decided to marry again.

"You remember that night, that Friday when we popped in, to The Lion, Gaz?" Gerry said, tapping his foot gently.

"Well while I was at the bar and you were over on the quiz thingy, Carla called over to me all friendly like, arm in arm with that waste of time Mick Waller!"

"Yeah go on, mate," I said intrigued and relieved Gerry was relaxed and ready to get everything off his chest at last.

"Well you know me and Waller have had our torrid moments to say the least."

"Yeah course. You mean that time he nearly slept with Sal...?" I said biting me tongue. A lot of animosity had gone on between Mick and Gerry over the years. Usually surrounding Sally and women who Mick Waller had hanging around him. But I thought I'd scuppered the moment by mentioning Sally (or almost mentioning her). Gerry got up and changed the Nick Drake CD, letting out a doleful sigh.

The remainder of our chat was all very chummy though, all to the mellowness of some classical collection. One of those 'Most Popular' type CDs. I wasn't one for music of any sort really, but Gerry had a real interest in a wide range of classical, pop, folk and the like.

"Do you like Vaughan Williams, Gaz, Lad?" he asked smiling broadly and then sitting to draw heavily on his Marlboro cigarette.

"Don't know, mate, who does she play for?" I said, smiling broadly.

"He was a keeper like you, when he returned from doing all that arty farty classical music caper," Gerry said, laughing out loud.

Laughter between us had been scarce since the 'Golden Time' thing, so I was feeling light hearted as Gerry offered me a Marlboro, lit himself another from the one he'd just had and said, "Yeah well, as you say, mate, after all that Sally business happened, I didn't have any time for the little shit, hated his guts to be reight about it, Gaz."

"Mmm go on, Gerry, I'm all ears," I said very interested.

"Anyhow, I haven't seen Mick Waller for donkey's years. So when Carla breezes into the Red Lion that neight and I'm thinking. 'What the hell's she doing in here?' Cause the last I knew 'Sal' and 'Carls' had buggered off back to the old bright lights of London Town, around spring 2007 I think it wa'?"

"Go on, Mr Potts, take your time," I said, pouring him another pint of lager from the large jug in the centre of the table.

"Yeah well," I says to Carls, "Oh hello, love, what you doin in here?"

It's a lovely surprise, throwing my arms around her and then ordering her a drink.

"'Pint of lager and one of those vodka pop efforts, Pat, for our Carly', I'd said to the landlord," Gerry said, as he relaxed back onto the seating on the houseboat, kicking off his slip on shoes, ones which are made of denim material with white soles.

"'What bloody vodka pop efforts? Gerry, I don't get you?' Pat had said. But I didn't have to explain as a white, cloudy bottle appeared at the side of my pint on the bar. One of the lasses who worked for Pat overheard and I sauntered off to join Carla at her table," Gerry said.

"Reight so Carla's in wi some others then?" I asked.

"Yeah, so I goes from the bar, up the couple of steps to the platform of seats and tables which overlooks the whole bar. There's no seat spare, the boozers packed up there and when I see Carla joined by Sally and Waller I'm glad not to be able to park me 'sen' amongst em."

Gerry began to become more subdued as he told me this. He gulped down more lager and finished his tale of woe.

"So I stands there like a reight lemon as I see Waller and Sally cooing over a tacky ring on her finger. Sally smiles at me; all 'smarmy' like and says,

'We're engaged, Gerry, aren't you pleased for us both?' Carly sat with Mick's son Bradley and they both smiled. They are embarrassed and look away before I walk away. That's when I joined you at the quiz thing machine."

EPILOGUE

AIMEE

I had just celebrated my ninth birthday when Mum told me the news about Dad.

We had a little party I remember at no.7. The little semi-detached I shared with Mum. Uncle Roy and our friend Lilly came along. I was still close friends with Leah, the girl I had first met at St Jude's Primary School. We both grew up together, staying very good friends to this day, so I invited Leah along too.

The next day I remember was a Friday. Uncle Roy and Lilly had bought me a lovely present. I love reading and they had kindly gifted me a book called *100 Great Lady Writers.*

I sat at the kitchen table that Friday just after my birthday. Mum was outside. She had taken to gardening since my Dad had been away, and spent many hours out there.

I was reading all about Enid Blyton who had written many famous children's books. I then heard Mum saying outside, "Oh thank you, Harry, have a nice day now."

But Mum didn't let on about the letter the postman had brought. Not until well after lunch time that day.

"Why didn't you tell me, Mum, as soon as Mr Harry had given you the post? Oh that's wonderful, what time is Dads train due, and when?"

My dad came home from Her Majesty's Prison in Waltham, South London on the 8th August 2013. A week to the day after my ninth birthday. He had spent near on three years inside.

For the next nine years my Dad found life very difficult. Before he had been arrested he had been a rough sleeper for three years. So add another three years he had spent in Waltham, meant he had not been a part of society at all for almost six long years.

Dad was a stranger when he first came back. Mum and I shared her bedroom, while he used the room I had always had. But Dad didn't just sleep in there, he made like, well my old bedroom became another cell. He rarely left. Mum would bring him his meals and try to coerce him out, but he was a stranger to us both.

Uncle Roy, Lilly, and some of his old pals he knew from his football days tried to help. Barry a lad he worked with on big decorating jobs in the past offered him work. But Dad just seemed lost and alone. Even with his own loved ones and friends he'd known all his life.

For the next four or five years until I was fifteen, Dad sometimes had to go into hospital. Mum was finding his behaviour stressful. We had tried everything we could in that first year he came back home. But all Dad was content, or able to bear was my old room. His days consisted of watching old football matches on the

DVD player, or reading books and newspapers. The only experience of a world outside was the fresh air blowing through the open window. Or he would stand staring longingly out of the window, watching Mum gardening or pegging out the washing.

Just after my fifteenth birthday though there was a breakthrough.

"Charlotte, Charlotte, love, you there?"

I heard Dad call out; his voice was cheery and normal. He hadn't spoken at all hardly in the years since he came back to live with us.

But just these few simple pleading words gladdened my heart. If he had spoken to us he rarely called us by our names.

By Christmas time that year Dad had made giant leaps forward. Uncle Roy and Mum told him of a place he might like to attend. The 'Starting Over' project was set up in Sheffield to help people. A day centre which assisted with all manner of problems. From the difficulties with alcohol and drugs, to giving a lot of support to ex-prisoners and the homeless like my Dad.

By my eighteenth birthday and Dad's 60th Mum had two special occasions to celebrate, the icing on both our cakes being also wonderful news. My efforts to become a published writer had been recognised. A publisher in London had finally made my dreams a reality. As for my dad, Gary, he had worked hard at 'Starting Over' to rebuild his life. He had been able to return to his work as a decorator, only a couple of days a week. But this had really boosted his waning confidence. Barry Denver the old workmate of Dad's had been able to gently teach

him all the old decorating skills, ones Dad had forgotten
and ones he had always adored.

In the Old Sun

HERMANN HESSE

TRANSLATED BY A. I. DU P. COLEMAN

Coyote Canyon Press

CLAREMONT, CA

Coyote Canyon Press
Claremont, California
www.coyotecanyonpress.com

Printed in the United States of America

Typeset in Swift

Library of Congress Cataloging-in-Publication Data

Hesse, Hermann, 1877-1962.
[In der alten Sonne. English]
In the old Sun / Hermann Hesse ; translated by A. I. du P. Coleman.
     pages cm
 "Translated from the German, In der Alten Sonne, by A[lexis] I[renée] du
P[ont] Coleman (1859-1926)."
 "One of Herman Hesse's earliest novels, In the Old Sun (In der Alten Sonne)
was completed in 1904. The story is of novella length and comes long before
the novels that were to make Hesse famous in the decades after World War II.
. . .The novel was first published in English in 1914 as Volume XIX of The Ger-
man Classics: Masterpieces of German Literature by the German Publication
Society"—Preface.
 Includes bibliographical references and index.
 ISBN 978-0-9890080-0-6 (alk. paper)
 1. Almshouses—Fiction. 2. Older men—Fiction. 3. Life change events—Fiction.
 4. Germany—Fiction. I. Coleman, Alexis Irénée Du Pont, translator. II. Title.

PT2617.E85I513 2013
833'.912—dc23

                        2013027043

IN THE OLD SUN

PREFACE

One of Herman Hesse's earliest novels, *In the Old Sun*
(*In der alten Sonne*) was completed in 1904. The story is of
novella length and comes long before the novels that were
to make Hesse famous in the decades after World War II.

In his early years as a writer, Hesse turned memories of his childhood home of Cawl—called "Gerbersau,"
after a favorite fishing spot on the Nagold River—into
a steady flow of *Novellen*, which kept his coffers replen-
ished; and the ranks of his reading public kept growing.
"In der alten Sonne," one of these recollective tales, was
first published in Hesse's *Nachbarn* (1908), a collection of
five works of fiction about the natives of his birthplace.

The novel was first published in English in 1914 in Volume XIX of *The German Classics: Masterpieces of German Literature* by the German Publication Society. The twenty illustrated volumes in the series were edited by Kuno Francke. The publishing house, which was created specifically for this series, went bankrupt soon after the German U-boat sinking of the British ocean liner Lusitania in 1915. One outcome of the Great War was that America's taste for German literature and culture dissipated overnight.

The translation by A[lexis] I[renée] du P[ont] Coleman is fairly modern. However, the text contains one slight error that merits correcting: the reference to one of the main characters, Heller, as a "sailmaker" is inaccurate; in the original German he is referred to as a *Seiler*, a rope maker. In addition to this correction, antiquated punctuation has been silently modernized.

Coyote Canyon Press is proud to bring back into print this "lost novel" by Hermann Hesse.

THE PUBLISHERS

IN THE OLD SUN

Whenever, in spring or summer or even early autumn, there comes a soft, pleasant day, just warm enough to make it agreeable to loiter in the open air, then the extravagantly crooked path that joins the Allpach road, just before you leave the last high-lying houses of the town, is a charming spot. On the serpentine windings of the path as it goes up the hill the sun always lies warm. The place is sheltered from every wind. A few gnarled old fruit trees give not indeed fruit but a little shade, and the border of the road, a green strip of smooth surf, entices you in the friendliest way by its soft curves to sit down or to stretch yourself at full length. The white path gleams in the sunlight as it climbs slowly and easily, sending a thin cloud of dust up to greet every farm wagon or landau or post chaise; and it gives a view over a steep huddle of dark roofs, broken here and there by the tops of trees, down into the heart of the town—to the marketplace, which indeed, seen from here, loses a good deal of its impressiveness, and appears only as a peculiarly foreshortened rectangle of irregular houses and curiously protruding front steps and cellar doors.

On such mild, sunshiny days the comfortable turf border of this lofty hill-climbing path is always oc-cupied by a small troop of resting men, whose bold, weather-beaten faces do not entirely harmonize with their tame and sluggish gestures, and the youngest of whom is well up in the fifties. They sit or lie at their ease in the warm greenness; they are silent, or carry on short, muttered conversations; they smoke short black pipes, and are continually spitting, with an air of con-tempt for the world, down the steep slope below them. The few workmen who pass by are sharply observed by them and critically placed; and each, according to the verdict, is greeted with a benevolent nod and "How are you, comrade?" or allowed to pass in disdainful silence.

A stranger who watched the old men lounging there, and inquired in the first street he came to about the odd collection of gray idlers, could learn from any child that they were known as the "Sun-Brothers." Many such strangers turned to look back once more at the weary group blinking in the sunlight, and wondered how they came to get such a lofty-sounding and poetical name. Some traveling enthusiasts felt a mysterious thrill at the name, and made out of the half-dozen gray loafers the surviving remnants of an almost extinct and very ancient community of worshipers of the orb of day. But the luminary after which the Sun-Brothers had been named had long ceased to shine in any sky; it was only the sign of a miserable tavern which had vanished several years before. Both sign and fame had disappeared, for the building served later as the city poorhouse, still harboring, indeed, numerous guests who had lived to see the setting of the sun taken down from the sign, and had acquired at its bar the reversion of their present shelter and guardianship.

The small house stood last in the steep lane and in the town, close to this sunny strip of turf. It offered a warped and weary front to the eye, as though it was a considerable effort to stand upright, and had nothing now about it to show how much merriment and cheerful clinking of glasses, joking and laughter it had seen, to say nothing of lively brawls and knife-play. Since the old pink paint of the front had grown pale and peeled off in cracked patches, the ancient abode of vagabonds corresponded accurately in its external appearance to its purpose, which is not always the case with municipal buildings in our day. Plainly and honestly, even eloquently, it gave every one to understand that it was a refuge for those who had made shipwreck of their lives and been left behind in the race, the desperate end of a narrow backwater from which no plans or hidden resources could ever work them out again into the stream of life.

Fortunately, little of the melancholy of such reflections was to be found in the circle of the Sun-Brothers. Rather, they—most of them—went on living after the fashion of their bygone days, puffed up their petty bickerings and fancies and amusements, friendships and jealousies, to the dimensions of weighty events and affairs of state, and took not each other but themselves as seriously as possible. In fact, they behaved as if it was only now, since they had extricated themselves from the noisy streets of the bustling world, that the chase was beginning; they carried on their insignificant affairs with a gravity and a tenacity which for the most part they had never been able to attain in their earlier activities. Like many another small collection of men, although they were ruled on the principles of absolute monarchy by the head of the institution and treated as mere imaginary existences without rights, they believed themselves to be a small republic, in which every free citizen had the same title to rank and position as another and was firmly determined never to allow himself to be too little esteemed, even by a hair's breadth.

The Sun-Brothers had this too in common with

other people, that they experienced the greater part of their destinies and satisfactions, their joys and sorrows, more in imagination than in tangible reality. A humorist might indeed have considered the difference between the life of these wrecks of humanity and that of busy citizens as consisting only in imagination, since both alike carried on their large and small affairs with the same busy gravity, and in the last resort an unfortunate inmate of the poorhouse might possibly not be much worse off in God's eyes than many a great and honored personage. But without going as far as that, it might well be contended that for the easygoing observer of life these Sun-Brothers were no unworthy object of contemplation, since human life, even upon a small stage, always offers an amusing drama and one well worth consideration.

The nearer the time approaches when the present generation will have forgotten the name of the old "Sun" tavern and the Sun-Brothers, and its poor and outcast members will be cared for in other places, the more desirable it is that there should be a history of the old house and its inmates. As a contribution to such a chronicle, these pages will narrate something of the life of the first Sun-Brothers.

In the days when the present young men of Gerbersau were still wearing short breeches or even dresses, and when over the door of the present poorhouse there still swung proudly from the pink facade, at the length of a wrought-iron arm, the tin sun which was its ensign, one day late in autumn Karl Hürlin came back to his native town. He was the son of Hürlin the locksmith in the Senfgasse, who was long since dead. He was a little more than forty, and no one knew him any longer, since he had wandered away as a very young man and had never since been seen in the town. Now, however, he wore a good, neat suit of clothes, a mustache and well-trimmed hair, a silver watch chain, a stiff hat and a high clean collar. He visited some of the former acquaintances of his family and a few old school friends, and bore himself in general as a man who had gone away and risen in the world, conscious of his value without over-emphasis. Then he went to the town hall, exhibited his papers, and declared that he intended to settle down in the place. After the necessary preliminaries had been accomplished, Herr Hürlin developed a busy and mysterious activity and correspondence, often took little journeys, and bought a piece of ground at the bottom of the valley. He began to build there, on the site of an oil-works that had burned down, a new brick house, a stable and coach house near it, and between the stable and the house a huge brick chimney. In the meantime he was seen now and then in the town taking his glass of an evening. At the beginning he was quiet and dignified, but after he had had a few glasses he would talk loud and emphatically, and made no secret of the fact that he had money enough to live a fine gentleman's life—but that one man was a thick-headed idler and another a genius and a man of business, that he belonged to the latter class and had no idea of sitting down to rest until he was able to write six ciphers after the figures that denoted his wealth.

Business people from whom he asked credit inquired into his history, and found out that up to that time he had never played an important part, but had been employed in various workshops and factories, rising finally to be a foreman. Lately, however, he had fallen into a tidy inheritance; and so people accorded him a certain measure of respect, and a few enterprising men put money also into his business. Soon, then, a moderately large and good-looking factory arose, in which Hürlin proposed to turn out certain rollers and other machinery required in the woolen industry.

Hardly was the place opened when its projector was sued by the same firm for which he had been overseer, on a charge of illegally representing as his own inventions and using some technical secrets which he had acquired there. He came out of the endless litigation without discredit but with heavy costs; he pushed his business with redoubled zeal, lowering his prices somewhat and flooding the country with advertisements. Orders were not lacking, the big chimney smoked night and day, and for a few years Hürlin and his factory flourished, and enjoyed respect and ample credit.

He had attained his ideal and fulfilled his old dream. It was true that in his earlier years he had made more than one attempt to acquire wealth, but it was the almost unexpected inheritance which had set him on his feet and enabled him to carry out his bold plans. Riches had not been his only aim; his warmest desires had all along tended toward the acquisition of a great and commanding position in the world. He would have been in his element as an Indian chief, as a privy councillor, or even as a master-huntsman; but the life of a factory-owner seemed to him both more comfortable and more independent. A cigar in the corner of his mouth and a grave and thoughtful smile upon his face, standing at the window or sitting at his desk to issue all sorts of orders, to sign contracts, to listen to suggestions and requests, to combine the wrinkled brow of the very busy man with an easy, comfortable manner, to be now unapproachably strict and now good-naturedly condescending, and at all times to feel that he was a leader of men and that much depended on him—this was his gift, which unfortunately had come only too late in life to full exercise. But now he had his desire to the full; he could do as he pleased, set people up or put them down, heave delightful sighs over the burden of wealth, and feel that he was envied by many. All this he enjoyed with a connoisseur's pleasure and with entire absorption; he wallowed in happiness, and felt that fate had at last given him the place that belonged to him.

In the meantime, the rival at whose expense he had grown great, made a new discovery, the introduction of which showed a number of the earlier products to be useless and turned out others much more cheaply. Since Hürlin, for all his self-confidence, was not a genius and understood only the externals of his trade, he descended at first slowly and then with increasing rapidity from his height of success, and finally reached a point where he was unable to conceal from himself that he was beaten. In desperation, he tried some daring financial expedients, through which he involved himself and a number of creditors with him in a complete and unsavory bankruptcy. He fled, but was caught and brought back, tried, and sent to jail; and when after several years he appeared once more in the town it was as a discredited and broken man who could not hope to make a fresh start.

For a while he found humble occupations; but in the sultry days when the storm was gathering he had developed into a secret drinker—and what had then been concealed and little regarded became now a public scandal. Dismissed from a small clerk's place for untrustworthiness, he became an insurance agent, and in this capacity took to visiting all the taverns of the neighborhood. He lost this employment too, and, when an attempt to peddle matches and pencils from house to house also failed to produce an income, he sank to be a charge on the community. In these years he had become suddenly old and wretched; but from the days of his ruined splendor he had retained a certain provision of small arts and an external manner which helped him over some rough places and still produced their effect in the lower class of public houses. He took with him to these places certain majestic and sweeping gestures and well-sounding habits of speech which had long corresponded to no inner reality, but on the strength of which he still enjoyed a standing among the good-for-nothings of the town.

At that time there was no poorhouse in Gerbersau; but people who were of no use to the community were maintained at a small provision from the town funds here and there in private families as lodgers. Here they were furnished with the absolute necessities of life and employed according to their capacity in small domestic labors. Since, however, all sorts of inconveniences arose from this system, and since no one at all was willing to receive the broken-down manufacturer, who enjoyed the hatred of the whole population, the community saw itself compelled to establish a special house as an asylum. And as at that particular moment the miserable old "Sun" tavern came under the hammer, the town acquired it and placed there as the first inmate, with a manager, Karl Hürlin. Others soon followed him; and they became known as the "Sun-Brothers."

Now Hürlin had long had close relations with the "Sun," since in the course of his decline he had frequented always lower and more wretched places, and finally had made his main headquarters there. He was expected among the daily visitors, and sat in the evenings at the same table with several boon companions who, when their time too came, were to follow him as despised paupers into the very same house. He was really glad to take up his abode there. In the days after the purchase of the property, when carpenters were busy transforming the old place to its new condition, he stood watching them from morning till night.

One mild, sunshiny morning he had arrived there as usual and taken up his position near the main door to watch the workmen at their task inside. One of the floors was broken and had to be relaid, the rickety stairs had to be patched up and provided with a firm balustrade, a couple of thin partitions put in. The town foreman was getting after the workmen, who were simulating great industry, and the schoolchildren were wandering from room to room. All this activity delighted old Hürlin. He looked on with cheerful interest, pretending not to hear the malicious remarks of the workmen; he plunged his hands into the deep pockets of his greasy coat, and twisted his charity trousers, much too long and wide for him, into various spiral forms in which his legs looked like corkscrews. He pulled continually at a chipped clay pipe, which was not lit but still smelt of tobacco. His approaching entry into his new abode, from which he promised himself a new and fairer existence, filled the old drunkard with delighted curiosity and excitement.

While he was watching the laying of the new stairs and silently estimating the quality and probable durability of the thin pine boards, he suddenly felt himself pushed to one side. As he turned in the direction of the street, he saw a workman with a large stepladder which with great care and many props he was attempting to set up on the sloping surface of the street. Hürlin betook himself to the opposite side of the street, leaned against a stone, and followed the activity of the workman with great attention. The latter had now set up his ladder and made it secure; he climbed it and began to scratch about in the mortar over the main door with a view of taking down the old sign. His efforts filled the ex-manufacturer with interest and also with pain, as he thought of the bygone days, of the many glasses of wine or spirits he had drunk under the now disappearing sign, and of the past in general. He took no little joy in observing that the iron arm was so firmly fixed in the wall that the workman had much trouble in getting it loose. Under the poor old sign there had been so many infernally good times! When the workman began to swear, the old man smiled; when he pulled and pushed and twisted and knocked, when he began to sweat and almost fell off the ladder, the spectator felt no little satisfaction. Finally he went away, and came back in a quarter of an hour with an iron saw. Hürlin perceived that now it was all over with the venerable ensign. The saw bit shriekingly into the good iron; after a few moments the arm began to droop, and finally fell with a rattle and a clang on the pavement.

Hürlin crossed the street. "I say, Mr. Workman," he begged humbly, "give me the thing; it's of no value now."

24

"Why? Who are you?" asked the fellow.

"I'm of the same religion," answered Hürlin entreatingly—"my father was a locksmith too, and I've been one in my time. Give it me, won't you?"

The workman picked up the sign and looked at it. "The arm is still good," he decided. "For its time it was not a bad piece of work. But if you want the tin thing, that's no use to anybody..."

He tore away the green tin wreath in which, with long since dimmed and lumpy rays about it, the golden sun had hung, and gave it to him. The old man thanked him and made off with his prize, to hide it in the elder bushes further up with a strange greed and pleasure in the thought of contemplating it. So, after a lost battle, a paladin might have hidden the insignia of fallen royalty, to preserve them for other days and new glories. When he returned, to recommence his inspection of the carpenters' work, the house struck him as changed and desolate because the sun was gone, and in its place over the door there was nothing but an ugly hole in the plaster.

A few days later, without much pomp or ceremony, the opening of the scantily-furnished poorhouse took place. A few beds had been put up; the rest of the furniture was the product of the tavern keeper's sale, except that a supporter of the scheme had decorated each of the three bedrooms with a Bible text surrounded by wreaths of flowers painted on cardboard. For the position of manager, when it was put up to competition, there had not been many applicants; and the choice had fallen upon Herr Andreas Sauberle, a widowed weaver of good repute, who brought his loom with him and continued to work at his trade—the position was not very remunerative, and he had no desire to become a Sun-Brother himself in his old age.

When old Hürlin had his room assigned to him, he at once began a minute examination of it. He found a window looking on the small courtyard, two doors, a bed, a chest, two chairs, a jar, a broom and duster; further, a shelf in the corner covered with oilcloth, on which stood a glass, a tin basin, a clothesbrush and a New Testament. He felt the stout bedclothes, tried the brush on his hat, held up glass and basin critically to the light, sat down experimentally on both the chairs, and decided that all was satisfactory and in order. Only the impressive text on the wall failed to meet with his approval. He contemplated it for awhile with a scornful expression, read the words, "Little children, love one another," and shook his bushy head discontentedly. Then he pulled the thing down, and with great care hung the old "Sun" sign in its place—the only piece of property he had brought with him to his new dwelling. But just as he did so the manager came in, and ordered him in a tone of rebuke to put back the text. He was going to take the tin sun with him to throw it away, but Karl Hürlin clung to it desperately, insisting with loud outcries on his rights of property, and finally hid the trophy, still growling, under his bed.

The life that began on the following day did not quite correspond to his expectations and at first did not please him at all. He was obliged to rise at seven and go to get his coffee in the weaver's quarters, then make his bed, clean his washbasin, polish his boots, and generally tidy up the room. At ten o'clock there was a piece of black bread for him, after which began the forced labor which he dreaded. A huge pile of wood had been dumped in the yard, which was all to be sawed and split.

As winter was still a long way off, Hürlin did not hurry himself with the wood. Slowly and carefully he laid a log in position, then he adjusted it with great accuracy, and considered awhile where he should begin to saw it, whether in the middle or on the right or the left. Then he applied the saw with the same care, laid it aside once more, spat on his hands and picked it up again. Now he took three or four strokes, cutting half an inch into the wood, but then drew the saw out again and examined it minutely, turned the screw, set it a little sharper, held it up and blinked at it for awhile, then heaved a deep sigh and rested for a time. Presently he began again and sawed a few inches into the wood; but he grew unbearably warm and stopped to take off his coat. This process he performed slowly and with reflection, and then looked about some time for a clean and safe place to put it. When it was properly bestowed, he began to saw once more—but not for long; the sun had come up over the roof, and shone directly in his face. This necessitated moving the log and the trestle and the saw, each separately, to another place where he could be in the shade. This exertion brought out the perspiration, and he was obliged to look for his handkerchief to wipe his forehead. It was not in his trousers pocket; he remembered having it in his coat, and so he strolled over to where he had put the coat, spread it out carefully, sought and found the colored handkerchief, wiped off the sweat, blew his nose, put the handkerchief away, folded the coat with great attention, and returned to his sawhorse much refreshed. Here he came to the conclusion that he had perhaps set the saw at too sharp an angle, and so he performed a new operation upon it which took some time, and finally, with much grunting, achieved the complete division of the log into two pieces. By this time the midday bells were ringing from the church-tower, so he quickly got into his coat, put the saw away, and went into the house to dinner.

"You're punctual, I'm bound to say that for you,"

remarked the weaver. The woman brought in the soup, after which there was some cabbage with a slice of bacon, and Hürlin fell to with a will.

After dinner the sawing was supposed to continue, but this he declined with emphasis. "I'm not accustomed to it," he said in an injured tone, and stuck to it. "I'm tired out, and must have a little rest."

The weaver shrugged his shoulders and said, "Do as you like—but a man that won't work mustn't expect any supper. At four o'clock there'll be bread and cider, if you've done your sawing—otherwise nothing more till the soup at night."

Bread and cider, thought Hürlin, and was confronted with a very serious problem. In the end he went out and picked up the saw again; but he shuddered at the thought of working in the hot midday hours, and he let the wood lie where it was. He went out in the street, found a cigar-stump on the pavement, put it in his mouth, and slowly covered the fifty paces to the bend in the road. There he stopped to take breath, sat down by the roadside on the fine warm turf, looked out over the many roofs and down to the marketplace, catching a glimpse at the bottom of the valley of his old factory, and dedicated this place as the first of the Sun-Brothers—the place to which afterward so many of his comrades and successors have come to lounge away their summer afternoons, and often mornings and evenings as well.

The gentle, beneficent contemplation of an old age free from cares and troubles, which he had promised himself in the poorhouse, and which that morning had faded under the pressure of hard work like a fair mirage, now returned gradually to him. His heart soothed by the feeling of a pensioner assured for the rest of his days from anxiety, hunger, and homelessness, he sat at his ease on the turf, feeling the pleasing warmth of the sun on his withered skin. He gazed over the scene of his former activities and misfortunes, and waited without impatience till someone should come who would give him a light for his cigar-stump. Shrill hammering from a workshop, the distant ring of the anvil in a smithy, the low rumbling of a faraway wagon came up to his heights with a little dust from the road and thin smoke from chimneys of all sizes, to show him that down in the town people were bravely toiling and sweating, while Karl Hürlin sat peacefully untroubled on his throne at a dignified distance from it all.

About four o'clock he came quietly into the room of the weaver, who was moving his shuttle regularly back and forth. He waited a while to see if there might not, after all, be some bread and cider, but the weaver only laughed at him and sent him away. He returned disappointed to his post of observation, growling to himself; there he put in an hour or more in a sort of half sleep, and then watched the coming of evening to the narrow valley. It was still warm and comfortable up there, but his cheerful mood departed little by little; in spite of his slackness, he began to get horribly bored doing nothing, and his thoughts returned incessantly to the snack that he had missed. He saw a tall glass full of cider standing in front of him, yellow and sparkling and perfumed with sweet herbs. He imagined how he would have taken it up, the cool round glass, and gulped down a good draught at the first, drinking then more sparingly. He gave an angry sigh as often as he woke from the delightful dream; and his anger went out against the pitiless manager, the weaver, the miserable skinflint, the little stumpy fellow, the oppressor, the seller of his soul, the poisonous Jew. After he had fumed enough at the manager, he began to be sorry for himself and fell into a tearful mood; but finally he made a resolution to work the next day.

He did not see how the valley grew paler and filled with soft shadows, and how the clouds took on a rosy tint; he was blind to the mild, sweet evening colors of the sky and the mysterious blue that came over the distant mountains. He saw nothing but that lost glass of cider, the toil that waited inevitably for him on the morrow, and the hardness of his lot. Those were the kind of thoughts he had been used to having when he had passed a day without getting anything to drink. What it would be like to have a glass of something stronger than cider was a thing he did not even dare to think about.

Stooping and languid, he made his way down to the

house at supper time, and took his seat ill-humoredly at the table. There was soup, bread, and onions, and he ate grimly as long as there was anything on his plate; but there was nothing to drink. After the meal he sat still disconsolately and did not know what to be at. Nothing to drink, nothing to smoke, no one to gossip with! For the weaver was working busily by lamplight, paying no attention to him.

Hürlin sat for a half hour at the empty table, listening to the click of Sauberle's machine and staring at the yellow flame of the hanging lamp, until he sank into an abyss of discontent, self-pity, envy, hatred and malice from which he neither sought nor found any way of escape. At last his silent anger and hopelessness grew too much for him. He raised his fist and brought it down on the table with a bang, rolling out a good German oath.

"Here!" said the weaver, coming over to him. "What's the matter with you? No cursing allowed where I am."

"Well, what in the devil's name am I to do?"

"Oh, you find the evening long? Then go to bed."

"There you are again! People send little children to bed at a certain time—not me!"

"Then I'll get a little work for you."

"Work? You're too free with your tyranny, you old slave driver!"

"Come, keep cool! But there—there's something for you to read." He put out a couple of volumes from the thinly-furnished shelves that hung on the wall, and went back to his work. Hürlin had no inclination to read, but he took one of the books in his hand and opened it. It was an almanac, and he began to look at the pictures. The first was a fantastically dressed ideal woman's figure depicted as an ornament for the title page, with bare feet and flowing locks. Hürlin remembered that he had a stump of lead pencil in his pocket. He took it out, wet it in his mouth, and drew two large round breasts on the woman's bodice, which he continued to emphasize, wetting his pencil again and again, until the paper was almost worn through. Then he turned the page and saw with satisfaction that the impress of his artistic design had gone through several other pages. The next picture on which he came illustrated a fairy story, and represented a kobold or some malicious spirit with evil eyes, a fierce mustache and a huge open mouth. Eagerly the old man wet his pencil again, and wrote under the monster, in large, legible letters, "This is Weaver Sauberle, the manager."

He was proposing to go through the whole book and deface and defile it all. But the next picture arrested his attention, and he forgot himself in studying it. It represented the explosion of a factory, and consisted of little beyond a huge mass of smoke and fire, around and above which whole or fragmentary human bodies, bricks, plaster, laths, and beams were flying through the air. This interested him, and led him into trying to reconstruct the whole story, and especially to imagine how the victims must have felt at the moment of being hurled into the air. There was a charm and a satisfaction in this for him which held him intent on the picture a long time; with all his egoism, he belonged to the numerous class who find more to think about in other people's fate, especially when it is strikingly illustrated, than in their own.

When he had exercised his imagination sufficiently on this exciting picture, he went on turning over the pages, and presently came to another that arrested him, though in quite a different way. It was a bright and cheerful picture—a pretty arbor, on the outer boughs of which hung a star for a sign. On the star sat, with ruffled neck and open beak, a little bird singing. Inside the arbor was to be seen, about a rough rustic table, a small group of young men, students or roving journeymen, who chatted and drank a good wine out of cheerful-looking bottles. To one side of the picture was visible a ruined castle raising its towers to heaven, and in the background a fair landscape stretched away, as it might have been the Rhine valley, with a river and boats and distant hills. The revelers were all handsome youths, merry and amiable lads, smooth-faced or with light youthful beards, who were evidently singing over their wine the praises of friendship and love, of the good old Rhine and of God's blue heaven.

At first this engraving reminded the morose and lonely man who looked at it of his own better days, when he, too, could call for a bottle of wine, and of the many glasses of good sound stuff which he had consumed. But by degrees the conviction stole over him that he had never been as happy and gay as these young revelers, even long ago in his light-hearted years of wandering, when he had taken the road as a journey-man-locksmith. The summer gladness in the arbor, the bright, good-humored faces of the young people made him sad and angry. He wondered whether it was all the invention of a painter, idealized and false, or whether there were in reality somewhere such arbors and such merry, carefree youths. Their smiling faces filled him with an envious longing; the more he looked at the picture, the more he felt as though he were looking for a moment through a small window into another world, into a fairer country and the life of freer and more gracious men than he had ever met in his life. He did not know into what strange kingdom he was gazing, nor that his feelings were those of people who read poetry, and get their pleasure in the beauty of the description from the reflection how much smaller and meaner the everyday reality is, passing into a slight, sweet sadness and longing. He did not well understand how to extract the sweetness from this kind of sadness, and so he shut the book, threw it angrily on the table, muttered a forced "Good night," and went up to his room, where the moonlight lay on bed and floor and chest and was reflected in the filled washbasin. The deep stillness, early as the hour was, the peaceful moonlight, and the emptiness of the room, almost too large for a mere sleeping chamber, awoke in the rough old fellow a feeling of unbearable loneliness, from which he escaped only after many muttered curses and some time later into the land of slumber.

There followed days in which he sawed wood and enjoyed his afternoon refreshment, alternating with days in which he was idle and did without it. He often sat up there by the roadside, full of poisonous, malicious thoughts, spitting down toward the town with all the bitterness of his unrestrained heart. The feeling he had hoped for, of being at peace in a safe haven, failed to visit him; instead, he felt himself sold and betrayed, and either made violent scenes with the weaver or brooded secretly in his own heart on the feeling of defeat and disgust and ennui.

Meanwhile the term for which board had been paid for one of the pensioners in private houses expired, and one day there came to the "Sun" as a second guest, the former rope maker, Lukas Heller.

While business reverses had made a drinker out of Hürlin, it was just the opposite with Heller. Nor had he, like the manufacturer, fallen suddenly from the height of showy riches; he had gone down slowly and steadily, with the necessary pauses and interludes, from an uncommon workman to a common vagabond. His good and energetic wife had been unable to save him; rather, the hopeless struggle had been too much for her, though she seemed much stronger than he, and she had died—while her good-for-nothing husband enjoyed rude health, played the fool for a few more years, and then, after he was ruined and dependent, went lazily on

40

with no apparent diminution of strength toward a ripe old age. Of course his conviction was that he had had bad luck with his wife as well as with the rope-making business, and that his gifts and performances had merited a better fate.

Hürlin had awaited this man's arrival with great eagerness, for he was growing daily more utterly weary of being alone. But when Heller appeared, the ex-manufacturer stood on his dignity and would scarcely have anything to do with him. He even grumbled because Heller's bed was put in the same room with his, although he was secretly glad of it.

After supper, since his comrade seemed disposed to be so grumpy, the rope maker took a book and began to read. Hürlin sat opposite him and threw occasional glances of suspicious observation at him. Once, when the reader could not help laughing at something amusing, the other was very much tempted to ask him what it was. But as Heller looked up from his book at the same moment, evidently willing to communicate the joke, Hürlin assumed a gloomy expression and pretended to be wholly absorbed in the contemplation of a fly that was crawling across the table.

So they sat the whole evening through. One read, looking up occasionally as if ready for a chat, the other watched him incessantly, only turning his eyes away haughtily when his companion happened to raise his. The manager worked away busily until late. Hürlin's face grew more and more sour and hostile, although he was really pleased to think he would no longer be alone in his bedroom. When ten o'clock struck, the manager spoke: "Now you might as well be going to bed, you two." Both rose and went upstairs.

While they were slowly and stiffly undressing in the dimly-lighted room, Hürlin thought the time had come to enter on an inquiry into the qualities of the companion in misfortune whom he had so long desired.

"Well, there's two of us now," he remarked, throwing his waistcoat on a chair.

"Yes," said Heller.

"It's a pig sty, this," the other went on.

"Oh—is it?"

"*Is* it? I ought to know! But now there'll be a little life in it—yes."

"Say," asked Heller, "do you take your shirt off at night or keep it on?"

"In summer I take it off."

So Heller took his shirt off too, and lay down in the creaking bed. Soon he began to snore loudly. But Hürlin's curiosity was not yet exhausted. "Are you asleep, Heller?"

"No."

"There's plenty of time…. Tell me, you're a rope maker, aren't you?"

"I was—a master rope maker."

"And now—?"

"And now—you must think a lot of me, to ask such silly questions."

"Oh, you needn't be so snippy! You old fool, you may have been a master rope maker, but that's not so much. I was a manufacturer—I owned a factory, do you understand?"

"You needn't shout at me—I knew that before. And after that, what did you manufacture?"

"What do you mean, after that?"

"You know what I mean—in jail."

Hürlin emitted a bleating laugh. "Oh, I suppose you're one of the pious kind—a psalm singer, eh?"

"I? That's the last thing! No, I'm not pious—but at the same time I've never been in jail."

"You wouldn't have been at home there. Most of the people there are fine fellows."

"O Lord! Fine fellows of your sort? You're right—I shouldn't have liked it."

"Some people have got to talk, whether they know what they're talking about or not."

"Just what I was thinking."

"Oh, come now, be a good fellow! What made you give up the rope making?"

"Oh, don't bother me! The business was all right, but the devil got into it somehow. It was my wife's fault."

"Your wife? Did she drink?"

"That would have been too much. No, I did all the drinking that was done, as is mostly the case, not the wife. But it was her fault just the same."

"Was it? What did she do?"

"Don't ask so many questions!"

"Have you got any children?"

"One boy—in America."

"Sensible fellow—a man's better off there."

"You'd think so—but he's always writing for money, the rascal! He's married, too. When he went away, I said to him, 'Friedel,' I said, 'good luck to you, and take care of yourself; do whatever you like—but if you marry, there'll be trouble.' Well, now he's got himself into it. Say, were you ever married?"

"No—but you see man can get into trouble even without a wife—don't you think so?"

"That's according to the man. I'd have my own shop today, if it hadn't been for my fool of a wife."

"H'm—!"

"Did you say anything?"

Hürlin was silent, and pretended to be asleep. He

had a premonition that if the rope maker ever got fairly started on the subject of his wife, there would be no end to it.

"Go to sleep, then, stupid!" cried Heller; the other did not allow himself to be drawn, but went on deliberately taking long breaths, until he really fell asleep.

Next morning the rope maker, who at sixty did not need so much sleep, was the first to wake. He lay for half an hour staring at the white ceiling. Then, although he had seemed so stiff in his movements the day before, he got out of bed as lightly and gently as a morning breeze, stole over in his bare feet to Hürlin's bed without making a sound, and began to explore the latter's clothes. He searched carefully through them, but found nothing except the stump of a pencil in the waistcoat pocket, which he took out and appropriated. A hole which he discovered in the left stocking of his companion he enlarged with the help of his two thumbs until it was of considerable size. Then he crept quietly back to his warm bed and did not move again until Hürlin was awake and up and had thrown a few drops of water in his face. Then he sprang up nimbly and got into his trousers. He did not, however, hasten to finish his toilette, and when the ex-manufacturer advised him to hurry, he said, "Oh, you go on down—I'll be after you in a minute." Hürlin did so, and Heller heaved a sigh of relief. He seized the washbasin and emptied the clean water out of the window—for he had a horror of washing. When he had avoided this distasteful process, he was soon ready to hasten down and get his coffee.

The making of the beds, tidying up the room, and polishing of shoes was attended to after breakfast, of course without undue haste and with plenty of pauses for conversation. The manufacturer found it all much more sociable and pleasant in company than alone; he began to have very friendly feelings toward his housemate, and to congratulate himself on the prospect of a lively and cheerful existence. Even the inevitable work seemed less terrifying than usual, and at the manager's summons he went down to the yard with Heller, not indeed swiftly but with an almost smiling countenance.

In spite of passionate outbursts on the part of the

weaver and his constant endeavors to conquer the reluctance of his charge, in the last few weeks the woodpile had shown very little alteration. It seemed almost as high and wide as ever—as though it had the blessed permanence of the widow's cruse of oil; and the little heap of sawed bits lying in a corner, barely a couple of dozen, looked like the result of a child's play, begun in a whim and as lightly thrown aside.

Now both the old men were to work at it. It was necessary to arrange for a combination, since there was only one sawhorse and one saw. After a few preparatory motions, sighs, and remarks, they conquered their inner reluctance and addressed themselves to their task. And now, unfortunately, Karl Hürlin's glad hopes showed themselves to have been idle dreams, for the manner of working of the two displayed the essential difference between them.

Each had his own special way of being busy. In both, alongside of the innate overmastering laziness, a remnant of conscience exhorted timidly to work; neither of them really wanted to work, but they wanted to be able to pretend to themselves at least that they were of some use in the world. They strove to attain this result in different ways; and in these two worn-out and useless fellows, whom fate had apparently destined to be brothers, there appeared an unexpected divergence of aptitudes and inclinations.

Hürlin was master of a method by which, though he did next to nothing, he was or seemed continually busy. The simple act of taking hold of a thing had come with him to be a highly developed maneuverer, owing to the way in which he associated with this small action a noticeable ritardando. Moreover, he invented and employed, between two simple motions, as between the grasping and applying the saw, a whole series of useless but easy intervening details, and was always concerned in keeping actual work as far as possible from contact with his body by such unnecessary trivialities. Thus he resembled a condemned criminal who devises this and that and the other thing that must be done and cared for and attended to before he goes to suffer the inevitable penalty. And so he contrived to fill the required hours with an incessant activity and to bring to them a pretense of honest toil, without having really accomplished anything that could be called work.

In this characteristic and practical system he had hoped to be understood and supported by Heller, and now found himself disappointed. The rope maker, in accordance with his inner character, followed an entirely opposite method. He worked himself up by a convulsive decision into a foaming fury, rushed at his work as though he did not care for life, and raged at it until the sweat flowed and the splinters flew. But this only lasted a few minutes; then he was exhausted—but he had appeased his conscience, and rested in motionless collapse until after a certain time the fury came upon him once more, and again he raged and steamed at his task. The results of this fashion of working did not notably surpass those of the manufacturer's.

Under these circumstances each was bound to be an offence and a hindrance to the other. The hasty and violent method of Heller, beginning at the wrong end, revolted the deepest feelings of the manufacturer, while his steady sluggish appearance of doing something was just as abhorrent to the rope maker. When the latter fell into one of his furious attacks on the job, Hürlin stepped back a few paces as if alarmed and looked on scornfully as his comrade puffed and panted, retaining, however, just enough breath to reproach Hürlin for his laziness.

"Look at him," he would cry, "look at him, the good-for-nothing loafer! You like that, don't you? to see other people doing your work! Oh yes, the gentleman is a manufacturer. I believe you've been quite capable of sawing away four weeks on the same log!"

Neither the offensiveness nor the truth of these reproaches stirred Hürlin up very much; but he did not let Heller get the better of him. As soon as the rope maker, wearied out, stopped to rest, he gave him back his accusations, finding a choice variety of ingenious terms of abuse to describe him, and threatening to hammer on his thick head until he should be in condition to mistake the world for a dish of mashed potatoes and the twelve apostles for a band of robbers. It never came, of course, to the execution of these threats; they were merely rhetorical exercises, and neither of the adversaries regarded them in any other light. Now and then they brought charges against each other before the manager; but Sauberle was wise enough to decline to interfere. "You fellows," he said crossly, "are not schoolchildren any longer. I'm not going to mix myself up with such squabbles—and there's an end of it!"

In spite of this, both of them came again, each for himself, to complain to him. Thereupon one clay the manufacturer got no meat for his dinner; and when he defiantly asked for it, the weaver said merely, "Don't get so excited, Hürlin; there must be penalties now and then. Heller has told me what you've been saying to him again this morning." The rope maker was not a little triumphant over this unexpected victory; but at supper the thing was reversed—Heller got no soup; and the two sly dogs realized that they were beaten at their own game. From that time on there was no more tale-bearing.

But between themselves they gave each other no

peace. Only now and then, when they crouched side by side on the turf by the roadside and stretched their wrinkled necks to look after the passers by, a temporary soul-brotherhood grew up between them, as they discussed the ways of the world, the weaver, the system of caring for the poor, and the wretchedly thin coffee in their abode, or exchanged their slender stock of ideas— which with the rope maker consisted in a conclusive psychology of women, with Hürlin in recollections of his travels and fantastic plans for financial speculations on a grand scale.

"You see, when a fellow gets married—" that was how Heller always began. And Hürlin, when it was his turn, opened with "If I knew anybody who would lend me a thousand marks," or "Once upon a time, when I was down at Solingen." He had worked there for three months many years ago; but it was remarkable how many things had happened to him or come under his notice in Solingen.

When they had talked themselves out, they sucked silently at their usually empty pipes, folded their arms about their thin knees, spat at irregular intervals on the road, and stared past the gnarled old apple trees down into the town whose outcasts they were, and whom in their folly they held responsible for their misfortunes. Then they became gloomy, sighed, made discouraged gestures with their hands, and realized that they were old and played out. This always lasted until their dejection changed again into malice, which generally took half an hour. Then, as a rule, it was Lukas Heller who opened the ball, at first with some little teasing remark.

"Just look down there!" he would cry, pointing toward the valley.

"What is it?" growled the other.

"You don't need to ask—I know what I see."

"Well, what *do* you see, in the devil's name?"

"I see the cylinder factory that used to be Hürlin & Schwindelmeier, now Dallas & Co. Rich men they are, I'm told—rich men!"

"Oh, go to the deuce!" growled Hürlin.

"Thank you!"

"Do you want to make me out a swindler?"

"No need to make you one!"

"You dirty old rope maker!"

"Jailbird!"

"You're an old drunkard!"

"Drunkard yourself! *You've* got no call to abuse decent people!"

"I'll knock in half a dozen of your teeth!"

"And I'll make you walk lame, my fine fellow. Bankrupt!"

Then the fight was on. After exhausting all the terms of abuse usual in the locality, the imagination of both rascals would invent new ones of the most audacious sort, until this capital too was used up, and the two fighting cocks would totter back to the house, exhausted and embittered.

Neither had any dearer wish than to get the better of the other and make him feel his superiority; but if Hürlin had the better brain, the rope maker was the more cunning—and since the weaver took no side, neither could claim a real triumph over the other. Both longed ardently to attain a position of superior consideration in the house; and they employed for this purpose so much energy, caution, thought, and secret obstinacy that with the half of these either of them, if he had put it to use at the right time, might have kept his bark afloat instead of becoming a Sun-Brother.

In the meantime the huge pile of wood in the yard had slowly become smaller. What remained had been left for another time, and other employments had been taken up. Heller sometimes worked by the day in the mayor's garden, and Hürlin was occupied under the manager's supervision in washing salad, picking lentils, shelling beans and the like—tasks in which he was not required to overexert himself, and yet could feel he was being useful. Under these conditions the feud between the two brethren seemed slowly healing, since they never worked together the whole day, and in their leisure hours each had enough to complain of and to report. Each of them imagined, too, that he had been selected for this particular work on account of special aptitudes which gave him a certain superiority over the other. So the summer drew along, until the leaves began to turn brown, and the evenings on which one could do without a light until nine o'clock were no more.

At this time it happened to the manufacturer, as he was sitting alone on the doorstep one afternoon and sleepily contemplating the world, to see a strange young man come down the hill who asked the way to the town hall. Hürlin was civil out of sheer boredom, went a couple of streets with the stranger, answered his questions, and was presented for his trouble with two cigars. He asked the next wagon driver for a light, lit one of them, and returned to his shady place on the doorstep, where with enthusiastic delight he gave himself up to the pleasure, long unknown, of smoking a good cigar. The last of it he put into his pipe and smoked it until there was nothing left but ashes and a few brown drops. In the evening, when the rope maker came from the mayor's garden, with, as usual, plenty to relate about the pear-cider and white bread and radishes he had had for his lunch, and how splendidly they had treated him, Hürlin also recounted his adventure with long-winded eloquence, to Heller's great envy.

"And what have you done with the cigars?" he asked at once with interest.

"Smoked them," said Hürlin, haughtily.

"Both?"

"Yes, you old simpleton, both."

"Both at once?"

"No, you fool, first one and then the other."

"Is that true?"

"Why shouldn't it be true?"

"Well," said the rope maker, who did not believe the story, quickly, "then I'll tell you something. You're a dumb ox, and a big one at that."

"Am I? And why?"

"If you'd put one by, you'd have had something for tomorrow. Now what have you got?"

This was too much for the manufacturer. With a grin he drew the remaining cigar from his breast pocket and held it before the eyes of the envious rope maker, in order to annoy him. "Do you see that? There—I'm not such a God-forsaken idiot as you think I am!"

"Oh, so you've still got one left! Let me look at it."

"Hold on! I don't know—"

"Oh, just to look at it. I'm a judge of whether it's a good one. You'll get it back right away." So Hürlin gave him the cigar. He turned it about in his fingers, held it to his nose and sniffed at it awhile, and said, as he reluctantly gave it back, "There you are—it's miserable cabbage leaf, the kind you get two for a kreuzer."

Then there arose a discussion as to the goodness and the price of the cigar, which lasted until they went to bed. When they were undressing, Hürlin laid his treasure on his pillow and watched it anxiously. Heller mocked him: "Yes, take it to bed with you! Perhaps it'll have little ones." The manufacturer made no reply; when his companion was in bed, he put the cigar carefully on the windowsill and went to bed too. He stretched himself luxuriously, and before he went to sleep still savored the enjoyment of the afternoon, when he had so proudly blown his smoke out into the sunshine, and when with the fragrance something of his former splendor and consciousness of greatness had returned to him. Just so in the old days, between his office and his workshop, he had pulled at his long cigar and sent up careless, lordly, captain-of-industry clouds. Then he went to sleep, and while his dreams conjured up the picture of his vanished greatness in all its glory, he stuck up his red and swollen nose into the air with the same proud contempt of the world as in his best days.

In the middle of the night, however, contrary to his custom, he suddenly woke up, and there he saw in the dim light the rope maker standing at the head of his bed, with a thin hand stretched out toward the cigar on the windowsill.

With a cry of rage he threw himself out of bed and barred the retreat of the malefactor. For a while no words were spoken; the two enemies stood facing each other, breathing hard but not moving, surveying each other with piercing glances of anger, uncertain themselves whether it was fear or excess of surprise that prevented them from having each other by the hair.

"Drop that cigar!" cried Hürlin at last, hoarsely. The rope maker did not alter his position. "Drop it!" shouted the other, and as Heller still did not move, he hauled off and would undoubtedly have given him a swinging blow if the rope maker had not ducked in time. In the movement, however, he dropped the cigar, Hürlin tried to grasp it, Heller trod on it with his heel, and with a light crackle it went to pieces. Then the manufacturer gave him a good one in the ribs, and the next thing a fair tussle was on. It was the first time they had come to blows; but their cowardice outweighed even their anger, and no serious damage resulted. Now one advanced a step, now the other; the two naked old men circled about the room without much noise as if they were performing some antique dance, each a hero and neither receiving a blow. This went on until in a favorable moment the manufacturer got his hand on his empty washbasin. He swung it wildly over his head and brought it down forcibly on the skull of his unarmed foe. It did him no particular harm, but the crash of the tin basin gave out a warlike and resonant sound that rang through the whole house. At once the door opened, admitting the manager in his nightshirt, who stood between scolding and laughing before the duelists.

"You're a pair of precious old rascals," he cried, "knocking each other about without a stitch on you, like a couple of old he-goats! Into bed with you—and if I hear another sound, you'll get something to be thankful for!"

"But he was stealing—" Hürlin began to shout, almost crying with rage and injured dignity, only to be instantly interrupted and ordered to keep quiet. The he-goats retreated muttering to their beds; the weaver listened a few moments at the door, and when he had gone all was still in the room. By the washbasin the fragments of the cigar lay on the floor; the pale summer night peeped in at the window, and over the two old rogues in their deadly hatred hung the flower-bedecked text, "Little children, love one another."

Hürlin extracted at least a minor triumph out of the affair the next day. He steadfastly refused any longer to share the same room with the rope maker; and after a stubborn resistance the weaver was obliged to give in and assign Heller another room. So the manufacturer once more became a hermit; and glad as he was to be rid of the rope maker's company, it preyed on his spirits to such an extent that he realized fully for the first time into what a hopeless *cul de sac* fate had thrust him in his old age.

The poor old man could make no cheerful prognostications. Formerly, however badly things went, he had at least been free; even in his most miserable days he had had a few pennies to spend at the tavern, and could set out on his wanderings again whenever he chose. Now he sat there, stripped of all rights and under discipline, never saw a copper that he could call his own, and had nothing before him in the world except to become older and feebler and, when his time came, to lie down and die.

He began to do what he had never done before—to look up and down from a high point of vantage on the Allpach road, over the town and along the valley; to measure the white high-roads with his eye, and watch the soaring birds and the clouds; to follow longingly with his eye the passing wagons and the pedestrians that went up and down, as a mourning exile from their company, left behind never to join them in their journeys. To pass the evenings, he accustomed himself now to reading; but from the edifying histories of the almanacs and pious periodicals he often raised a distant and depressed eye, feeling that he had nothing in common with such people and events, recalling his young days, Solingen, his factory, the prison, the joyous evenings in the old "Sun," and coming back always to the thought that now he was alone, hopelessly alone.

Heller, the rope maker, cast sidelong and malicious glances at him, but after a time attempted to reestablish intercourse with him. When he met the manufacturer out at their resting place, he would occasionally put on a friendly expression and greet him with "Fine weather, Hürlin! I think we shall have a good autumn, don't you?" But Hürlin merely looked at him, nodded wearily, and made no sound.

In spite of all this, some thread would have gradually spun itself to link the two perverse creatures together; out of his very melancholy and disgust, Hürlin would have grasped as for dear life at the first comer, if only to get rid now and then of the wretched feeling of loneliness and emptiness. The manager, who was displeased by the manufacturer's silent moroseness, did what he could also to bring his two charges together. But finally a sort of salvation, if a dubious one, came to all three. During the month of September there came to the house at short intervals two new inmates—two very different ones.

One was called Louis Kellerhals; but this name was not known to anybody in the town, for Louis had borne for decades the appellation of Holdria, whose origin is undiscoverable. When, many years before, he had become a pensioner of the community, he had been placed with a friendly artisan, where he had been well treated and counted as a member of the family. The artisan had now, however, died with unexpected suddenness; and since his protégé could hardly be reckoned as part of the inheritance he left, it was necessary for the poorhouse to receive him. He made his entrance with a well-filled linen bag, a huge blue umbrella, and a green wooden cage containing a very fat common sparrow. He seemed little upset by his change of quarters; he came in smiling and beaming with cordiality, shook every one heartily by the hand, spoke no word and asked no questions, brimmed over with delight and kindliness when any one spoke to him or looked at him, and even if he had not long been a well-known figure, could not have concealed for a quarter of an hour the fact that he was a harmless and well-meaning imbecile.

The second, who made his appearance about a week later, brought with him not less joyful benevolence, but was not weak in the head; on the contrary, though harmless enough, he was a thoroughly cunning fellow. His name was Stefan Finkenbein; he was a member of the wandering beggars' dynasty of the Finkenbeins, long well known throughout the whole town and neighborhood. Of this complicated family two branches had settled in Gerbersau, counting several dozen members. They were all without exception sharp-witted fellows; yet none of them had ever come to any notable fortune, for it was an inseparable characteristic of their nature to love to be free as the birds and to rejoice in the humor of having no possessions.

The said Stefan was still below sixty, and enjoyed perfect health. He was rather thin, indeed, and his limbs were delicate; but he was always well and active, and it was something of a mystery how he had been able to foist himself upon the community as a candidate for a place in the poorhouse. There were plenty of people in the town older, more wretched, and even poorer. But from the very foundation of the institution he had been consumed by a desire to enter it; he felt himself a born Sun-Brother, and would and must be one. And now there he was, as smiling and amiable as the excellent Holdria, but with much less extensive baggage—for besides what he wore on his back he brought nothing but a stiff Sunday hat of old-fashioned respectable elegance, well preserved in shape if not in color. He bore himself as a lively social light, accustomed to the world. Since

Holdria had already been assigned to Hürlin's room, he was put in with Heller, the rope maker. He found all his surroundings good and praiseworthy, except that the taciturnity of his companions did not please him. One evening before supper, as all four sat outside the door, he suddenly began: "Say, Mr. Manufacturer, are you always so mournful? You're a regular streamer of crape!"

"Oh, don't bother me!"

"Why, what's the matter with you? Why do we all sit round, anyhow, so solemnly? We could have a drop of something good once in a while, couldn't we?"

Hürlin gave ear for a moment with delight, and his tired eyes glistened; then he shook his head despairingly, he turned his empty pockets inside out, and assumed an expression of suffering.

"Oh, I see—no coin!" cried Finkenbein, laughing. "Good gracious, I always thought one of those manufacturer fellows had something jingling in his purse. But today's my first day here, and it mustn't go dry like this. Come on, all of you—Finkenbein's still got a little capital in his breeches for a time of need."

Both the mourners sprang to their feet at once. They left the weak-minded old fellow sitting where he was, and the three others tottered off at a quick pace toward the "Star," where they were soon sitting on a bench against the wall, each with a glass in front of him. Hürlin, who had not seen the interior of a tavern for weeks and months, was full of joyous excitement. He breathed in the atmosphere of the place in long draughts, and absorbed his liquor in short, economical, timid sips. Like a man awakening from an evil dream, he felt that he had been restored to life again, and welcomed home by the familiar surroundings. He brought out once more all the half-forgotten free gestures of his old sporting days, banged thunderously on the table, snapped his fingers, spat at ease on the floor and scraped noisily over it with his foot. Even his manner of talking showed a sudden change, and the full-toned words of power that recalled the days when he was a commanding figure rang out from his blue lips with something of the old brutal security.

While the manufacturer thus renewed his youth

and sunned himself in the afterglow of his old accomplishments and his bygone happiness, Lukas Heller blinked thoughtfully at his glass and felt that the time had come to repay the proud fellow for all his insults, and especially for the dishonoring blow with the tin washbasin on that memorable night. He kept quite still and waited watchfully for the right moment.

Meantime Hürlin, as had always been his custom, began with the second glass to listen to the conversation of his neighbors at the next table, to take part in it with nods and grunts and play of expression, and finally to interject an occasional "Oh yes" or "Really?" He felt himself quite restored to the beautiful past; and as the conversation at the adjoining table grew more animated, he turned more and more to face the speakers and, as his old habit was, soon plunged with fire into the clash of conflicting opinions. At first the other men paid no attention to him, but presently one of them, a driver, suddenly cried out, "Lord, it's the manufacturer! What's the matter with you, you old rascal? Be good enough to hold your tongue, or I shall have to tell you something!"

Hürlin turned away, cast down; but the rope maker gave him a dig in the ribs and murmured eagerly to him, "Don't let that fellow shut you up! You tell *him* something, the smarty!"

This encouragement at once inflamed the sensitiveness of the manufacturer to new self-consciousness. He banged on the table defiantly, moved a little nearer to the speaker, threw bold glances at him, and spoke in his deep chest-tone, "A little more manners, if you please. You don't seem to know how to behave."

Some of the men laughed. The driver answered, still good-humoredly, "Look out for yourself, manufacturer! If you don't shut up, you may get more than you bargain for."

"I don't have to," said Hürlin with emphatic dignity, once more egged on by a nudge from the rope maker; "I belong here just as much as you do, and have got as good a right to talk as the next man. So now you know!"

The driver, who had just paid for a round of drinks at his table and so felt entitled to take the leading position, got up and came over, tired of the altercation. "Go back to the poorhouse, where you belong!" he said to Hürlin; then he took him, shrinking in alarm, by the collar, dragged him over to the door, and helped him through it with a kick. The others laughed, and were of the opinion that it served the disturber right. The little incident was closed, and they resumed their important discussion with oaths and shouts.

The rope maker was happy. He persuaded Finkenbein to order one more little drink, and, recognizing the value of this new associate, he bent all his endeavors to establish friendly relations with him, to which Finkenbein yielded with a quiet smile. He had once undertaken to beg where Hürlin was already at work on the same line, and had been forcibly warned off by him. In spite of this, he bore no grudge against him, and declined to join in the abuse which the rope maker now poured out upon the absent man. He was better adapted than these who had sunk from happier circumstances to take the world as it came and to tolerate people's little peculiarities.

"That's enough, rope maker," he said protestingly. "Hürlin's a fool, of course, but by long odds not the worst in the world. I'm glad we've got him to play the fool with up there."

Heller accepted the correction and hastened to adapt himself to this conciliatory tone. It was now time to leave, so they moved along and got home just in time for supper. The table, with five people sitting at it, had now an imposing appearance. At the head sat the weaver; then on one side came the red-cheeked Holdria next to the thin, decayed and miserable-looking Hürlin. Opposite them sat the cunning rope maker with his scanty hair, and the merry, bright-eyed Finkenbein. The latter entertained the manager successfully and kept him in good humor, from time to time addressing a few jokes to the imbecile, who received them with a flattered grin. When the table had been cleared off and the dishes washed, he drew a pack of cards from his pocket and proposed a game. The weaver was disposed to forbid it, but finally gave in, on condition that the game should only be for love. Finkenbein burst out laughing.

"Of course, Herr Sauberle. What else could it be for? I was born to millions, but they were all swallowed up in the Hürlin stock—excuse me, Mr. Manufacturer!"

They began to play, then, and for awhile the game went along merrily, broken only by numerous jokes from Finkenbein and by an attempt at cheating on the rope maker's part, discovered and exposed by the same clever person. But then the rope maker began to feel his oats, and displayed a tendency to make mysterious allusions to the adventure at the "Star." At first Hürlin paid no attention; then he made angry signs to stop him. The rope maker laughed maliciously, looking at Finkenbein. Hürlin looked up, caught the disagreeable laugh and wink, and suddenly realized that Heller had been the original cause of his ejection and was now making merry at his expense. This struck him to the heart. He made a sour grimace, threw his cards on the table in the middle of a hand, and could not be persuaded to continue the game. Heller saw what was the trouble; he discreetly said nothing, and redoubled his endeavors to place himself on a friendly footing with Finkenbein.

Thus the fat was in the fire again between the two old antagonists; and the discord was all the worse because Hürlin was now convinced that Finkenbein had known of the plot and helped it along. The latter bore himself with unchanged geniality and comradeship; but since Hürlin now always suspected him, and took in bad part his jesting designations as "the Councillor," "Herr von Hürlin," and the like, the Sun-Brotherhood soon split into two parties. The manufacturer had soon grown accustomed to the silly Holdria as a roommate and had made him his friend.

From time to time Finkenbein, who from some hidden source or other had now and then a little money in his pocket, proposed another secret excursion to the tavern. But Hürlin, strong as the temptation was for him, kept a stiff front and never went with them, although it hurt him to think that Heller was thus getting the better of him. Instead, he stayed at home with

Holdria, who listened to him with radiant smiles or with large, troubled eyes when he growled and cursed or when he drew fanciful pictures of what he would do if any one lent him a thousand marks.

Lukas Heller, on the other hand, cleverly kept up his relations with Finkenbein. It was true that in the early days he had exposed the new friendship to grave peril. One night, in his characteristic fashion, he had gone through his roommate's clothes, and found thirty pfennigs in them which he appropriated. The victim of the theft, who was not asleep, watched him calmly through his half-closed eyelids. Next morning he congratulated the rope maker on his dexterity, paid him high compliments, requested the return of the money, and behaved as though it had all been a good joke. In this way he got Heller completely in his power; and although the latter had in him a good, lively comrade, he could not pour out his complaints against Hürlin to him quite as unrestrainedly as could Hürlin to his ally. And his diatribes against women soon became wearisome to Finkenbein.

"That's all right, rope maker, that's all right. You're like a hand-organ with only one tune—you haven't any changes. As far as the women are concerned, I dare say you're right. But enough of anything is enough. You ought to get another waltz put in—anything else, you know—otherwise I wouldn't care if someone stole you."

The manufacturer was secure against such declarations. This was well enough, but it did not make him happy. The more patient his auditor was, the deeper he sank in his melancholy. A few times the sovereign lightheartedness of the good-for-nothing Finkenbein infected him for half an hour to the extent of reviving the grand gestures and sententious utterances of his golden days—but his hands had grown stiff, and the words no longer came from his heart. In the last sunshiny days of autumn he sometimes sat under the decaying apple trees; but he never looked on town and valley now with envy or desire. His glance was faraway and strange, as if all this meant nothing to him and was out of his range. As a matter of fact, it did mean nothing to him, for he was visibly breaking up and had nothing more ahead of him.

His decline came on him very swiftly. It was true that soon after his downfall, in the thirsty days when he first grew well acquainted with the "Sun," he had grown very gray and begun to lose his agility. But he had been able for years to get about and drink many a glass of wine and play the leading part in a conversation in the tavern or on the street. It was only the poorhouse that had really brought him to his knees. When he had rejoiced at his installation there, he had not realized that he was cutting off the best threads of his life. For he had no talent for living without projects and prospects and all sorts of movement and bustle; and it was when he had given in to weariness and hunger and abandoned himself to rest that his real bankruptcy took place. Now there was nothing left for him but to wait a little while until his life went out.

The fact was that Hürlin had been too long accustomed to tavern life. A gray-haired man cannot break off old habits, even when they are vicious, without damage. His loneliness and his breach with Heller had helped to make him increasingly silent; and when a great talker grows silent, it means that he is well on the road toward the churchyard.

It is a depressing sight when an artist in life, even on a small scale, who has grown old in elegant trifles and ostentation and self-seeking, instead of coming to a sudden end in a fight or as he goes home at night from the tavern, must live on to grow melancholy and end as a dabbler in the sentimental reflections which have always been foreign to him. But since life is incontestably a powerful composer, and thus cannot be accused of senseless caprices, there is nothing for it but to listen to the strains it produces, to admire, and to think the best of it. And after all there is a certain tragic beauty in the thing when such a spirit, that has been spoiled and left raw and then beaten down, rebels at the very end and clamors for its rights, when it flutters its awkward wings and, since nothing else is left, insists on having its fill of bitterness and complaint.

There was much now that came to rub and gnaw at

this rude, ill-trained soul; and it became evident that its earlier stubbornness and self-control had rested upon insecure foundations. The manager was the first to realize his condition. To the pastor, on one of his visits, he said with a shrug of his shoulders: "One can't really help being sorry for Hürlin. Since he's been looking so down in the mouth, I don't make him work; but it's no use— that's not what's troubling him. He thinks and studies too much. If I didn't know his sort too well, I should say it was just his bad conscience, and serve him right. But that's not all of it. There's something gnawing at him from inside—and at his age a fellow can't stand that long. We shall see." After this the minister sat now and then with Hürlin in his room, near Holdria's green bird cage, and talked to him of life and death, and tried to bring some light into his darkness—but in vain. Hürlin listened or not as his mood was, nodded or hummed, but spoke no word and grew constantly stranger. Once in a while one of Finkenbein's jokes would appeal to him, and he would give a dry laugh or beat on the table and nod approvingly; but immediately afterward he would sink into himself again to listen to the confused voices that claimed his attention and tormented him without his being able to understand them.

Outwardly he only seemed quieter and more plaintive, and all treated him much as before. The imbecile alone, even if he had not been himself so feeble-minded, was capable of understanding Hürlin's condition and his gradual decline and feeling a certain horror at the sight; for this friendly and peaceful soul had become the manufacturer's constant companion and friend. They sat together by the wooden cage, put their fingers in between the bars for the fat sparrow to peck at, lounged of a morning, now that winter was coming on, by the half warm stove, and looked at each other with as much comprehension as if they had been two sages instead of a pair of poor hopeless fools. You can see at times two wild beasts locked in together looking at each other in just the same way; according to the mood of the observer, their gaze will seem dull, amusing, or terribly moving.

What troubled Hürlin most was the humiliation he

had experienced at the "Star" through Heller's instigation. At the very table where he had long sat almost daily, where he had spent his last penny, where he had been a good customer, a friend of the house and a leader in debate, there landlord and guests alike had looked on and laughed when he was kicked out. He had been forced to feel in his own bones that he belonged there no longer, that he did not count, that he had been forgotten and struck off the list and had no longer any shadow of rights.

For any other scurvy trick he would have avenged himself on Heller at the first opportunity. But now he did not even bring out the accustomed words of abuse that sat so easily on his tongue. What could he say to him? He had been entirely right. If he were still the same man as of old, still worth anything, they would not have dared to turn him out of the "Star." He was done for, and might as well pack up and go.

And now he looked forward to contemplate the destined straight and narrow path, an uncounted series of empty, dull, dead days, and at the end of it death—of which he thought sometimes with longing, sometimes with an angry shudder. It was all settled, nailed down and prescribed, unmistakable and inevitable. There was no longer any possibility of falsifying a balance sheet or forging a paper, of turning himself into a stock company, or by tortuous paths through bankruptcy sneaking out again into life. He was no longer a firm or a name— only a worn-out old man before whom the abyss of the infinite opened in all its terror, with the grisly skeleton silently grinning at him to cut off his retreat. Though the manufacturer had been accustomed to many different kinds of circumstances and knew how to find his way about in them, these were different. Now he tried to wave them away with weak gestures of his old arms, now he buried his face in his hands, shut his eyes, and trembled with fear of the inescapable hand which he felt descending to grasp him.

The good-hearted Finkenbein, coming gradually to suspect that all manner of ghosts were closing in upon the manufacturer, sometimes gave him an encouraging word, or clapped him on the shoulder with a consoling laugh. "I say, Mr. Councillor, you oughtn't to study so much. You're quite clever enough—in your time you got the best of plenty of rich and clever people, didn't you? Don't be cross, millionaire—I don't mean any harm. It's just my little joke—man; think of the holy text up over your bed!" And he would spread out his arms with a pastoral dignity, as if in blessing, and recite with unction, "Little children, love one another!"

"Or, wait a bit," he would say again, "we'll start a savings bank, and when it's full we'll buy from the town its shabby poorhouse, and take the sign out and make the old "Sun" rise again, so as to get some oil into the machine once more. What do you say to that?"

"If we only had five thousand marks—" Hürlin would begin to reckon; but the others would laugh, and he would break off, heave a sigh, and return to his brooding.

When winter had fully come, they saw him getting more silent and restless. He had fallen into the habit of wandering in and out of the room, sometimes grim, sometimes with a look of terror, sometimes with one of watchful cunning. Otherwise he disturbed nobody. Holdria often kept him company, falling into step with him in his incessant wanderings through the room, and answering to the best of his powers the glances, gestures, and sighs of the restless rambler, always fleeing before the evil spirits whom he could not escape because he carried them with him. Since all his life he had loved to play a deceiver's part and played it with varying luck, now he was condemned to play through to a desperately sad end with his harlequin-like manners. He played miserably and absurdly enough—but at least the role corresponded to himself, and the former *poseur* now for the first time came on the stage without his mask, not to his advantage. The realization of the infinite and the eternal, the longing for the inexpressible, innate in this soul as in others but neglected and forgotten through a whole lifetime, found now, when it swelled up, no outlet, and attempted to express itself in grimaces, gestures, and tones of the strangest kind, absurdly and laughably enough. But there was a real power behind it all; and the uncomprehending desire for death was certainly the first great and, in the higher sense, rational movement which this small soul had known for years.

Among the queer performances of a mind off the track was this, that several times a day he crawled under his bed, brought out the old tin sun, and offered it a foolish reverence. Sometimes he carried it solemnly before him like a holy monstrance; sometimes he set it up in front of him and gazed upon it with entranced eyes, sometimes he smote it angrily with his fist, only to take it up tenderly the moment after, caress it and dandle it in his arms before he restored it to its hiding place. When he began these symbolic farces, he lost what little credit for intelligence remained to him among his housemates, and was put down with his friend Holdria as an absolute imbecile. The rope maker especially regarded him with undisguised contempt, played tricks upon him and humiliated him whenever he could, and was seriously annoyed that Hürlin seemed to take so little notice of him.

Once he got the tin sun away from him and hid it

in another room. When Hürlin went to get it and could not find it, he roamed through the house for a while, looking for it repeatedly in many different places; then he addressed impotent threatening speeches to all the inmates, the weaver not excepted; and when nothing did any good, he sat down at the table, buried his head in his hands, and broke into pitiful sobbing which lasted for half an hour. This was too much for the sympathetic Finkenbein. He gave a mighty box on the ear to the terrified rope maker, and forced him to restore the concealed treasure.

The tough frame of the manufacturer might have resisted for many more years, in spite of his almost white hair. But the desire for death, though it was working almost unconsciously in him, soon found its way out, and made an end to the ugly tragicomedy. One night in December it happened that the old man could not sleep. Sitting up in bed, he gave himself to his desolate thoughts, staring at the dark wall, and seemed to himself more forsaken than usual. In this mood of weariness, fear, and hopelessness he finally rose from

In the Old Sun

87

his bed without knowing too well what he was doing, unfastened his hempen suspenders, and hanged himself with them to the top of the door-jamb. So Holdria found him in the morning, and the imbecile's cry of horror soon brought the manager. Hürlin's face was just a little bluer than usual, but it was impossible to disfigure it very much.

It was a terrible surprise, but its effect was of short duration. Only Holdria whimpered softly over his bowl of coffee; all the others knew or felt that the manufacturer's end had come at a good time for him, and that there was no real cause for regret or horror. And then no one had loved him.

Of course a few penny-a-liners made haste to investigate the interesting case, and communicated to the readers of their cheap papers, together with the necessary moralizings, the fact that the not unknown bankrupt Karl Hürlin had made a rather suitable end as a suicide in the poorhouse.

* * *

When Finkenbein had come as the fourth inmate, there had been some complaints in the town about the way in which the newly-founded institution was rapidly filling. Now one was gone from the number; and though it is true that paupers are usually of robust constitution and reach a good old age, yet it is also true that a hole seldom stays as it is, but seems to eat into the stuff around it. So it was here, at any rate. The colony of good-for-naughts was scarcely founded before consumption seemed to set in and went on working.

For the moment, indeed, the manufacturer seemed to be forgotten, and all went on as before. Lukas Heller took the lead in the little community, so far as Finkenbein would allow him the primacy, made the weaver's life a burden to him, and managed to put off half of the little work he was supposed to do upon the willing Holdria. He was thus comfortable and cheerful; he began to settle down as in a warm nest, and resolved not to worry under these delightful circumstances, but to live many years for his own pleasure and the annoyance of the citizens. Now that Hürlin was gone, he was the eldest of the Sun-Brothers. He made himself quite at home, and had never in his life found himself so much in harmony with his environment, whose secure though not luxurious peace and idleness left him time to stretch himself easily and to contemplate himself as a respectable and not altogether useless member of society—of the town, and of the world as a whole.

It was otherwise with Finkenbein. The ideal picture of a Sun-Brother's life which his lively fancy had painted in such glowing colors was far different from what he had found the reality to be. To be sure, to all appearance he was still the same light-footed jester as of old; he enjoyed his good bed, the warm stove, the solid and sufficient food, and seemed to find no fault with anything. He continued to bring back from mysterious trips into the town a few small coins for drink and tobacco, in which he generously allowed the rope maker to share. He was seldom at a loss to know how to pass the time, for he knew every face up and down the road, and was a general favorite—so that at any house or shop door, on bridge or steps, by wagons or push-carts, as well as at the "Star" and the "Lion," he was able to enjoy a gossip with any one who came along.

In spite of all this, he was not at ease. To begin with, Heller and Holdria were hardly satisfying daily companions for him, who had been used to intercourse with livelier and more rewarding people; and then he found increasingly burdensome the regularity of this life, with its fixed hours for rising, eating, working, and going to bed. Finally, and this was the main point, the life was too good and comfortable for him. He was trained to alternating days of hunger with days of feasting, to sleeping now on linen and now on straw, to being sometimes admired and sometimes browbeaten. He was used to wandering where the spirit moved him, to being afraid of the police, to having little games with the fair sex, and to expecting something new from each new day. He missed this poverty, freedom, movement and continual expectation here; and he soon came to the conclusion that his admission to the house, which he had procured by many stratagems, was not, as he had thought, his master stroke but a stupid mistake with troublesome and lasting consequences.

If these views led Finkenbein to a somewhat different end from the manufacturer's, it was because he was in everything of an opposite temperament. Above all, he did not hang his head, nor did he let his thoughts travel ceaselessly over the same empty field of mourning and dissatisfaction, but kept them fresh and lively. He paid little heed to the future, and danced lightly from one day into the next. He captivated the weaver, the simpleton, the rope maker Heller, the fat sparrow, the whole system on their humorous side, and had retained from his old life the comfortable artist's habit of never making plans or throwing out anchors for wishes or hopes beyond the situation of the moment. So it proved successful for him now too, since he was assured and provided for the rest of his days, to lead the life of the birds and the flies; and it was a blessing not only to him but to the whole house, whose daily life acquired through his presence a touch of freedom and of elegant hilarity. This was distinctly needed—for

Sauberle and Heller had, of their own resources, hardly more than the good-natured simpleton Holdria to contribute to the cheering and adornment of the monotonous existence.

So the days and weeks flowed along quite tolerably, and if it was not always jolly, at least there were no more quarrels or discords. The manager worked and worried himself thin and weary; the rope maker greedily enjoyed his cheap comfort; Finkenbein shut one eye and lived on the surface of things; Holdria positively bloomed in eternal peace of mind, and increased daily in amiability, in appetite, and in weight. It would have been an idyllic state of things—but the haggard ghost of the dead manufacturer was hovering about. The hole was destined to grow larger.

And so it came to pass that on a Wednesday in February Lukas Heller had some work to do in the woodshed in the morning; and since he was still unable to work in any other way than by fits and starts and with long pauses, he came and sat down under the archway in a perspiration and developed a cough and a headache. At midday he ate hardly half his usual amount; in the afternoon he stayed by the stove shivering, coughing, and swearing; and by eight in the evening he went to bed. Next morning the doctor was sent for. This time Heller ate nothing at all at dinner; a little later fever set in, and in the night Finkenbein and the manager had to take turns in watching by him. The next thing was that the rope maker died, recalcitrant, envious, and by no means patient or tranquil; and the town was rid of one more pensioner, which no one regretted.

It was to have better luck still. In March an unusually early spring set in, and things began to grow. From the big mountains to the ditches by the roadside, everything became green and young; the high-road was peopled by precocious chickens, ducks, and traveling journeymen, and birds of every size flitted through the air on joyous wings.

The growing loneliness and stillness of the house had been getting more and more on Finkenbein's nerves. The two deaths seemed to him of evil omen, and he felt more than ever like the last survivor on a sinking ship. Now he took to smoking and leaning out of the window by the hour into the warmth and mild spring feelings. A sort of ferment was in all his limbs and around his still young heart, which felt the call of spring, remembered old days, and began to consider whether there might not be a spring for it too amidst all this universal growing, sprouting and well-being.

One day he brought back from the town not only a packet of tobacco and the latest news, but also, in a worn bit of waxed cloth, two new pieces of paper which were adorned with beautiful flourishes and solemn official blue seals, but which had not been procured at the townhall. How should such an old, bold traveler not understand the delicate and mysterious art of producing on nicely written documents any desired stamp, either old or new? It is not every one who knows how to do it; it takes skillful fingers and much practice to extract the thin inner skin of a fresh egg and spread it out without a wrinkle, to press on it the stamp of an old certificate of residence and permit to travel, and to transfer it cleanly from the damp skin to a new paper.

One fine day, then, Stefan Finkenbein disappeared without any flourish of trumpets from the town and the district. He took for his journey his tall, stiff hat, and left behind as a sole memento his old woolen cap which was almost falling to pieces. The officials instituted a small and considerate investigation. But since rumors soon came in that he had been seen in a neighboring jurisdiction, alive and happy in a favorite resort of his kind, and since nobody had any interest in bringing him back without necessity, standing in the way of whatever happiness he might find, and continuing to feed him at the town's expense, it was decided to abandon the investigation and allow the free bird, with the best of wishes, to fly wherever he chose. Six weeks later came a postcard from him to the weaver, in which he wrote:

"Honored Herr Sauberle: I am in Bavaria. It is not so warm here. Do you know what I think you'd better do? Take Holdria and his sparrow and show him off for money. We might both travel on that. Then we might hang up Hürlin's sign. Your true friend, Stefan Finkenbein, Doorknob-gilder."

There might have been more trouble in the almost empty nest of fate, but the last Sun-Brother, Holdria, was too innocent and of too sedentary a disposition. Fifteen years have gone by since Heller's death and Finkenbein's disappearance, and the imbecile still dwells, sound and rosy-cheeked, in the former "Sun." For a while he was the only inmate. The numerous personages who were qualified held back discreetly and timidly for some little time; the terrible death of the manufacturer, the swift taking off of the stout rope maker, and the flight of Finkenbein had gradually shaped themselves into a widely-known theory, and surrounded the dwelling of the imbecile for as much as six months with bloody legends and tales of horror. After this period, however, need and laziness again brought several guests to the old "Sun," and since that time Holdria has never been alone. He has seen some curious and tiresome brothers come, share his meals, and die; and at this moment he is the senior of a company of seven, without counting the manager. Any warm, pleasant day you may see the whole company on the turf by the side of the hill-road, smoking their stumpy pipes and with weather-beaten faces and various feelings looking down on the town which in the meantime has grown considerably up and down the valley.

CPSIA information can be obtained at www.ICGtesting.com
Printed in the USA
LVOW06s1512300915.

456349LV00001B/2/P